ALSO BY L.M. BROWN

Debris

TREADING THE UNEVEN ROAD

Lorna M. Brown

Fomite

Burlington, VT

ISBN-13: 978-1-944388-80-5
Library of Congress Control Number: 2018967667
Fomite
58 Peru Street
Burlington, VT 05401

For My Sisters
Susan, Rachel, Elizabeth
with love

An old man cocked his ear upon a bridge;
He and his friend, their faces to the South,
Had trod the uneven road.

—W.B Yeats

Contents

The Lady on the Bridge 1

The Sacred Heart 17

The Taste of Salt 57

The Shape of Longing 67

The Wrong Man 88

Blackbirds 116

The Man on Sea Road...129

Amends 154

White Trout 173

THE LADY ON THE BRIDGE

BERNADETTE NOTICED THE ADDRESS book on her way out of the bedroom on the floor amid her husband's crumpled clothes. It probably fell out of his jeans, as he undressed the night before. He'd come home late again. She'd been asleep, though it had taken a long time to drift off because of the rain lashing against the windows and her worry that the river might overflow. The February rains had brought the level dangerously high. Last night, she'd lain in bed and imagined the water breaking its banks to cover the field and inch towards her house on the other side of the narrow road. She felt the same keen nervousness reaching for her husband's book as she did with the thought of the flooding. It was not the first time she saw his book, which was usually kept in his jeans pocket, or occasionally thrown on his night stand, but it was the first time she considered looking through the pages. The rain had stopped hours ago and she listened for the drum of the shower. Her husband might have been humming, though she had an idea that he had stopped that habit years ago. In any case, all she heard was the beat of the water and the buzzing in her ears. The book had a worn leather cover and fit easily into her palm. Her hands shook as she flicked it open. Mike was the name she'd heard often. It was Mike's idea to play snooker on Tuesday and Thursday, Mike who wanted to meet at the weekend. She'd never met Mike. Their nights out were boys' nights and besides Bernadette didn't like nightlife and detested pubs. Whenever she suggested having Mike over for dinner there was always some kind of excuse. She'd begun to hate the sound of the name and had started to imagine a faceless woman whenever Marcus mentioned him.

There was a chance that her husband had written the woman's real name in his address book but she didn't think he would do that. He was careful. He made sure to come home every night, and bar some loose change, she hadn't found anything in his pockets. With his shirts pressed to her face she never detected any perfume so she was left with nothing but a niggling feeling that would not leave. There was only one entry under M and no address, just a local number. She went to her office next door to get a pen and paper, while saying the number in her head over and over. The address book, she'd put back on the floor exactly where she'd found it.

Inside the cover of a romance, she wrote Michele and then the digits. Later she would cross the name out and write Vicky. The names she gave the woman she thought her husband was seeing depended on her mood. While he was out that evening she considered dialing the number but she was afraid the woman had caller ID. If she was with Marcus, she would know not to answer. Either that or Marcus would answer and say, "Bernadette what are you doing?"

She would end up the guilty one. When she'd confronted him, he'd laughed at her and said, "You can't seriously think I'm having an affair."

"Yes," she'd wanted to say, "I do." But she had nothing to go on, and he was already looking at her as if there was something wrong with her.

He'd said, "There's no other woman." Then, "Okay," as if that was simply the end of it.

She thought of using the phone box in the village but didn't want to go when it was dark. The idea of being illuminated by passing headlights made her feel dirty. Her mother had wandered through the village at night and Bernadette had heard about it when she was too young to think of such things. Ann Lavin had been a name spoken often in the town, Bernadette's drunken legacy.

She waited until Saturday morning to walk to the phone box while Marcus slept. The sidewalk was narrow and the pavement cracked in places. Above her the sky was clear of clouds. Still the cold forced her to put her hands in her coat pockets. A mile from her house and to her right, a bridge with high iron railings led to Main Street. At one time the village would have been busy with traffic going to and from Galway and Dublin, but that was before the bypass brought quietness to the area and a lull to the shops. Close to the bridge, Bernadette heard the gush of the river as it rushed towards the sea. The statue of Our Lady was just ahead of her. The grotto was set in an alcove with a low semi-circular wall. Once, Bernadette saw her mother inebriated and holding onto Our Lady's white arms, while she'd whispered to the cracked stone face. Since then, Bernadette had never been able to get close to the grotto without feeling an icy sensation.

She crossed to the bridge. Below her the river pushed against a lone fisherman standing to his knees in water. His silver line glinted in the sun. On the opposite side of the road was the Dun Maeve hotel. The rooms were rarely rented. The proprietor made his money with the bar patrons and the lunches popular with the men from the quarry. The front doors were closed, but Bernadette knew some people had already knocked on the back door and gained entry. Ten a.m., and her mother was probably there. She'd deserted her family when Bernadette was ten. There were nights when Bernadette remembered her father waiting at the kitchen table for his wife, but he never spoke of that time and refused to mention his wife's name.

Bernadette would sometimes see her mother walking the village. She was a small sad looking woman who hadn't spoken to her daughter in years. The sight of her made Bernadette nervous, and she avoided her mother by building her house on the opposite side of the village and shopping in Sligo town. But she looked out for her too. If weeks had gone by without a sighting, she'd get worried, only to be let down when she saw her mother's figure darting through the streets.

The phone box was at the far end of Main Street outside Spar, the local supermarket. Bernadette had copied the phone number three times and knew it off by heart. Still she held the paper tight in her hands. She felt confident until the door closed behind her, and she thought of the person she might reach on the other end. Numbers for taxis were stuck on the body of the phone. 'Josie is a slut' was written in black ink. 'I luv Tommy' was etched in pen. Bernadette dialed without knowing what she would say. Her throat had gone dry. She closed her eyes when the phone on the other side started to ring. For a moment she thought no one was at home and the relief surprised her. Then at the last second, just before she was about to give up, the ringing stopped, and she heard a groggy hello. The voice was deep and without doubt male. She exhaled with relief. "Hello?" He repeated.

She hung up. Her heart was pounding when she fed more coins into the phone and dialed again.

"Hello?" He sounded awake now and annoyed.

She said, 'Is this Mike?"

And he countered with, "Who is this?"

She told him it was Marcus' wife.

After a few moments, he said, "Oh," Then, "Yes, I'm Mike, is everything okay?"

She said, "Not really."

She could hear his steady breathing while her free hand played with the cord of the phone. He cleared his throat, and she was afraid he'd hang up so she said the first thing that came to mind. "Do you ever watch that show where couples have to guess the right answers about each other? You know the presenter gives certain scenarios and asks what they think their partner would do, or they ask about the things they like. It's on Saturday nights."

He said yes.

She said, "Every time I watch it I think we'd do terrible at it. I think of all the things I don't know, like his favorite movie. I can't remember what that is now. If they asked what my husband's favorite movie is, I'd have to tell them I don't know."

There was a moment of silence, before he said, "Blade runner or Platoon, it depends."

"Oh," she said. She wanted to say thanks but the surprise was too great. Her shoulders sagged and memory of her mother made her stand straighter. Bernadette's fingers tapped the glass of the phone box. She said, "Are you married?"

He said, "I used to be."

She asked if he lived alone.

He said, "Why are you phoning me?"

"I feel like there's something I should know."

"Why are you asking me?"

She told him because it's easier. "I don't see your face."

"I always thought that was the worst things about phone calls, to have nothing but the voice. It's like being blind."

She said, "What do you look like?" And he laughed, though she'd been serious. He told her he had to go and said, "Goodbye Mrs. Blake."

"Bernadette," she said and he said okay Bernadette.

"Don't tell Marcus I called, please."

For a moment, he said nothing and then he said okay.

The next Saturday she was up early and waited at her kitchen table for the morning to reveal a dry blustery day. On her walk to the phone box, her face tingled with the cold. She crossed to the bridge without a glance at the grotto where her mother sought redemption one afternoon. When Mike answered the phone, he didn't sound as groggy as he had the previous week. The silence after his 'hello' made her nervous. If she hadn't spent hours rehearsing what to say she would have clammed up, but she managed to tell him, "I took my husband bird watching once." She paused, unsure and shaky. She wasn't used to volunteering information like this.

He said. "Go on."

She told him it was terrible and he chuckled.

"It wasn't Marcus' fault," she said. "He might have enjoyed it if I didn't keep asking if he was okay. It was impossible to forget his presence. He's like that, or I'm like that. I don't know which."

"What do you mean?"

"I might have been too conscious of anyone. I'm used to being alone," When she'd uttered the last word she felt something drift down the line. It could have been tension rising between them, or maybe he'd just sat up in bed. Maybe it was nothing but the quiet unsettling her. All those things she wanted to say during the week were forgotten. She'd even messed up what she wanted to say about bird watching. She'd wanted to tell him about Marcus mistaking a reed for a bird. He asked, "Why bird watching?"

Relief made her lean on the glass. She told him about the first time she cycled to the bay. She saw a bird standing by the shore. It was beautiful, but it was the stillness that got her. For hours it didn't move and for hours she didn't think of anything else but that bird.

"What kind of bird was it?"

"A grey heron," she said and imagined he nodded.

She asked what he liked to do, and thought he would say snooker. Instead she felt that tension again and he said, "I'm sorry, I have to go."

She didn't tell him not to tell Marcus. When he went out the following Tuesday, she was nervous and scared. She imagined him coming back angry and demanding to know what she'd been doing behind his back. There was no way she could explain finding Mike's number or why she'd phoned him from the phone box. It was deathly quiet while Marcus was out. For three or four days, it hadn't rained and she missed the hammering on her window. With the lights off in the bedroom she could see the dark strip of river on the other side of the field but not the movement so it looked like a wide gap in the world. She was still awake and pretending to read when Marcus came in. "How was it?" she asked. She thought her voice shook, but he didn't seem to notice. The moment he smiled, she knew Mike hadn't told him anything. Happiness let her slide down the bed. She closed her eyes while her husband undressed, and wondered why Mike hadn't said anything to Marcus. Was it to protect her? Was it because Mike wanted their conversations to continue? Or because it would have sounded strange to say

'I've been talking to your wife.' Maybe he'd simply forgotten to mention her.

The following Saturday, she was excited to ask him. In his omission, she'd felt an element of subterfuge. She'd imagined that they might talk with more ease. She would take her time and tell him that she and Marcus were 21 when they got married.

She'd tell him about the night they'd sat in the gloomy silent house she'd shared with her father. Marcus had turned to her suddenly and said why not? And she said why not what? And he'd said get married and she said, "Because I might end up like my mother."

He'd laughed and told her, "Not with me you wouldn't. We could protect each other." And she'd studied him, and asked if he was serious. She couldn't remember saying yes. She remembered hugging him, and the relief from getting out of the house that she'd been cleaning since she was ten years old because her father wouldn't let a stranger inside the door.

Saturday morning, Marcus was still asleep when she closed the front door gently behind her. The day was cold with low lying clouds, so it seemed as if there was no gap between land and sky. In her bubble, with her gaze on the pavement she remembered how scared she used to be of the cracks and how her father had made her stand on them one by one. The river was empty of fishermen. A bus on its way to Galway was parked outside the supermarket. At one stage Bernadette would have loved to jump on any bus and get away but she'd married young and got a job in her father's company and the longing was buried in her chest now.

She felt a tinge of nervousness as she put her coins into the phone box. During the week she'd kept her 20's and 50's and each time she put a coin away she thought of something to say. The phone rang out and she heard. "Sorry I'm not in right now, please leave a message."

She hung up and tried again. She imagined Mike would come rushing to the phone, and the click of the answering machine brought a heavy disappointment.

The previous two Saturdays, when she'd heard Mike's voice she'd forgotten where she was. Now she felt conspicuous and too aware of everything. The butcher across the road was hanging meat in the window. She never liked the look of him in the white bloodstained apron. Behind her, Faith Wheeler was probably unlocking the door of her bakery. Her small figure might be taking the space in the doorway. Bernadette folded up slightly. She moved closer to the phone, as if this could hide her. Despite the grey day, she wore no hat over her long red hair. Faith was probably staring at her now and wondering why Bernadette was in the phone box when she had a phone at home. Faith had always been kind. After Bernadette's mother left, she had often knocked on Bernadette's door to ask how she was. They'd gone for walks because Bernadette had never wanted to let anyone enter their house where remnants of her mother existed in the small things she'd left behind that Bernadette hadn't the heart to throw out. When Bernadette got married, she left a bowl of her mother's belongings in the bathroom cabinet, clips and lost ear-rings, forgotten make-up and an old tissue with the faint shape of a mouth in lip-stick. She wondered if the bowl was still there but had not checked in years.

Bernadette didn't leave a message. She dialed Mike's number. Again, she got the voice mail and felt her stomach drop. Her chin quivered. Nollaig Sheehy, her father's secretary was going into Spar. Bernadette turned her head away before the wave. She didn't want anyone to approach her and was slow to get out of the phone box.

At the far end of the bridge, she stood staring at Our Lady. The statues slender hands were raised towards the sky. Bernadette crossed the road. She must have been curious about the statue when she was a young child, but she couldn't remember ever standing within its alcove. During the warmer months, there would be an array of flowers growing around the circular low wall but now the only color was the blue of Our Lady's robe and eyes. Bernadette was surprised with how sorrowful those eyes looked now.

That night, when Marcus said he was meeting Mike, Bernadette was shaken by the jealousy that rose in her. She imagined the two of them talking in the pub while she sat alone at home.

"Can I come?" she asked. He smiled and said no. With the fall of her face, he reminded her that she hated pubs. No matter where she was she had the irrational idea that her mother would appear. Also she was afraid to drink in case she might slip into her mother's lonely life. From the kitchen table, she watched Marcus put on his jacket. She wanted to grab his hand and plead with him not to go. But she couldn't, because she was afraid that she would break down and tell him that she had gone behind his back to speak to his friend. And she was terrified to admit that there was something troubling her. A dark cloud had spread in her chest but she didn't know why. It could have been from her disappointment with not speaking to Mike and the embarrassment every time she considered the evidence of her phone calls. Four times, she tried to call. Four times, he would have heard her breathing and frustrations. Yet she thought it was more than this, something bigger than the phone box and their conversations. It had started with the quickness Mike had said "*Platoon* or *Blade Runner*," and had spread because Mike had made her want to talk.

Every morning, she woke thinking of the things she wanted to say to him. At work, Bernadette sat at her desk and stared at her phone, imagining Mike in his house. She wondered if he would answer should she call and if he would hang up when he heard her voice. She might have dialed his number if her father's office wasn't next door. She couldn't phone from home, not with the chance that Mike would answer thinking it was Marcus and feel tricked by her. She started to imagine what Mike looked like. She pictured him bald for some reason, maybe a little older than her and Marcus. There was gentleness to his voice that she associated with age. She imagined he had small hands holding the phone. Maybe, he was a small man, unassuming, not like the broad-shouldered figure of her husband whose presence was so powerful it often left her tongue tied. Marcus had changed from the teenage boy she'd first met, and the young man she had married. Or maybe she had not noticed the fierceness of his black eyes, and the quietness that permeated from him until a distance had been set.

She'd wanted to tell Mike that for the first years of their marriage Marcus had hardly stepped outside the house. Because of his old friend Patrick Lenhihan, Marcus had been distrustful and scared. There was a fight she wanted to say. It was over some pool game, though she didn't know much because Marcus didn't like to talk about it. All she knew was Patrick beat Marcus. Marcus had a badly bruised face when he first approached Bernadette, and Patrick left town soon after. She wanted to tell Mike that for a long time Marcus didn't talk to many people other than her. Then he'd joined the gym and everything started to change but she didn't mind at first because he was happier than he'd been in years.

Marcus was up when she left the house the following Saturday morning. She slipped out while he was in the shower. It was raining heavily but she passed the two cars parked side by side in her driveway. The river looked thick and black that day. Our Lady was washed out. Water dripped from her hands and down her face. The silver railings on the bridge sparkled. Close to the phone box, she saw Faith's bakery was open. She knew the billboards with specials would be kept by the kitchen until the rain stopped. Bernadette used to write them out on weekend mornings, back when the village was busy and Faith opened early for breakfast. It had been Bernadette's first job.

She felt invisible as she slid into the phone box. She'd always loved the rain for the feeling of being obscure. Mike answered the phone at the first ring. She said hello. She wanted to ask where he was last week but his voice was gruff when he said, "What do you want Bernadette?"

She didn't know what to say. Her body felt heavy all of a sudden. Her mouth was dry but she didn't want to hang up. She waited for him to do so and was surprised when he didn't. His breathing was hardly detectable, as if he was keeping the phone a little from his face. Maybe he was expecting her to scream. The thought amused and eased her. She didn't know how to broach the subject of Patrick Lenhihan. So she said the first thing that came to mind, "Do you know my mother wore black on our wedding day?"

He said nothing. She leaned against the glass. "She wasn't invited for many reasons, but her house was on the way to the church, and she stood at the gate with a long black dress. I told Marcus it was just coincidence, but I never really thought so."

After a while, he said, "What did you think?"

When she said she didn't know, he said she must think something, otherwise why bring it up.

She said. "Sometimes I think that she cursed us, like the bad fairy Godmother."

She thought he might laugh but he didn't, and it scared her. She said, "Does Marcus think that too?"

Mike said, "He thinks she's cruel."

She remembered he'd said that to her years ago when they'd first gotten together. They'd talked about the cruelty of people like her mother and Patrick Lenhihan.

She said, "Did he tell you about Patrick Lenhihan? Did he

tell you about his best friend who beat him up over a game of pool? Did he talk about that cruelty?"

Mike didn't say anything. His breathing had gotten louder. She wondered if he was getting mad, and if so why he listened. Was it pity that kept him on the line or curiosity?

"Mike?" she urged.

And he told her yeah he knew about Patrick. The knowledge sat like a lump in her stomach. Marcus had hardly talked about Patrick. The beating seemed information too intimate to divulge to anyone else. It made Bernadette want to slide down against the glass and curl up.

Mike said, "You shouldn't phone me anymore. You should talk to Marcus."

She wanted to tell him that was impossible. She could wait for hours to talk to Marcus, and forget everything she wanted to say, because of the way he looked at her. But she felt Mike drifting away and it scared her. She asked, "Why can't I talk to you?"

He said, "Because, that's the way it is."

There was a pause, before he said, "I'm sorry," and hung up.

Long after he was gone, she took the phone from her ear. Rain was sliding down the glass in small streams and made her think of the grey kitchen in her father's house. She remembered how the light had shone on his bald spot when he'd waited at the table. And she thought Mike had probably never sat like that. He didn't understood what it was like to lose. If he did, he wouldn't say, "That's the way it is."

She was sure that at the kitchen table, while her father had waited for his wife, he'd prayed that 'this was not the way it is'. And even now, walking home while the darkness spread through her chest, she was inclined to deny the truth about her husband and Mike's relationship and say, 'this is not the way it is'.

At the end of the bridge, she paused with the rain running down her face before crossing to Our Lady. There was no one on the street, when Bernadette reached out to touch the cool stone of the statue's face. She was tempted to rest cheek against cheek and wondered what her mother had whispered years ago, if she'd pleaded for forgiveness from a husband who'd had enough, or for understanding from her daughter who hid whenever her mother approached.

She wondered what Mike had told Marcus about the phone calls. He must have spoken of it, "You should talk to Marcus," he'd said. She imagined Marcus hanging up the phone from Mike now, and walking to the living room window to watch the rain slide down the window and wait for her return.

THE SACRED HEART

AT THREE YEARS OF age, Dick Hurley slipped out the back door of his home unnoticed by his mother. His two story house was one of forty in a housing estate on the outskirts of a small village. The frames of the windows were brown and the grass was getting long. His mother didn't like gardening. She was too shy to be in view of her neighbors and preferred to polish and clean inside. With two boys she still managed to have the house in good shape. She always started in the kitchen with the dusting of the Sacred Heart and worked outwards to the rest of the house. Friday, she'd start cleaning as early as 6am in preparation for Henry Morrison's visit. He was in his fifties and soft-spoken with huge hands and pockmarked skin. In most houses he'd be asked into the kitchen but not in Mrs. Hurley's. She was nervous and anxious around him and he hated having to put her through the ordeal. He'd gone to the council to ask if Mrs. Hurley could send a check in every week in order to save them the discomfort, but was told no because he needed to inspect the place.

Henry was collecting rent the morning Dick ran from his home. The boy was quick on his feet, the kind to jump into action without a second thought. None of the neighbors saw him on that cool September morning, but through the years they could easily imagine the wiry figure of the boy dashing down the road. When their neighbors thought of Dick Hurley as a three year old, they thought of him with the same dark brooding eyes and pent up energy from too many ideas in his head. To know Dick made it hard to think he had ever been an innocent directionless little boy. No, he had a plan. He'd probably been preparing his escape for days. There was no telling what might have happened and where he might have gotten to if his little brother hadn't been around.

Where Dick took after his father, dark and skinny with wide set navy eyes and a thin thoughtful mouth, Enda Hurley was fair like the mother with brighter eyes and a quiet way about him. No one knew where he got his broad shouldered body from. As a baby, he'd been pudgy and slow to walk. His granny and aunts were forever pinching his cheeks, not only because the round fatness of them was irresistible but because of his brothers reaction. Dick was quick to slap the hands away and shout, "My bruver don't like that."

It was Enda who got his mother's attention that morning. He'd pulled at her skirts until she had no choice but to stop her hoovering. Henry Morrison was coming from the widow Maggie's house. Her bungalow was around the corner from the Hurley's. Their back gardens were separated by a wooden fence and Maggie's kitchen window would have framed the boy's escape, but she'd been staring at the dirty tea cups on her table. If Henry was more observant he might have seen the boy darting onto the street, but Henry had turned the corner thinking of Maggie's slender waist. He didn't know anything was amiss until he'd reached the Hurley fence and saw the mother running from the back of the house with the youngest boy in her arms.

"He's gone, he went out the back door!" she shouted at Henry. She didn't wait for an answer. Her face was red and her cheeks wet, but he didn't think she was aware of the tears. There was fury to her that let her hold the large boy in her hands as if he weighed a feather. She wore brown slippers and Henry would say later that it was the saddest thing he'd ever seen. "I can't explain it, just this screaming woman and a boy missing and then these brown slippers that were so out of place." She ran on to the end of the street and her voice rose to fever level when she saw Dick. She put Enda on the ground. He stood on thick wobbly legs and held onto the mother's arms. She said something to the toddler, and then took off. The boy was starting to whimper when Henry reached him. Henry saw Dick running like a bat out of hell and the mother after him. Dick had a good head start. He'd gotten passed the row of two-story houses and was flying past the field with the stone pathway and bench. Henry watched enthralled. He would tell this story for years; how Dick seemed to be running for his life, while the blonde boy hardly moved a muscle. His mouth had dropped open and his eyes were watery, but he made no attempt to run after his mother. He didn't call for her, though Henry could sense the tension in the little body. Had the mother and brother disappeared from view, there would have been screams. Dick didn't hesitate for a second or turn to look at his mother calling him.

"Dick, stop this minute. Dick. Stop, Dick."

Dick was running by Lavin's construction with not a glance at the diggers and trucks held behind the iron gates. He was going straight for the main road. It might have been the river from there.

"I swear to God he knew exactly what he was doing," Henry would say in the pub, and everyone in the estate would know and repeat the story of Dick Hurley singled minded and determined at three years old and Enda Hurley's stillness and obedience.

"She fell over him. She was going that fast and the two landed on the ground. I have no idea how the boy wasn't hurt, if she was any bigger than a twig he might have been and wee Enda didn't move an inch until she started limping back to him."

"Aw sure look, you couldn't get two any more different," was the usual response. Yet there was no denying the brothers shared a pensive nature. Dick could be seen as conniving from the way he looked and sized up the world. Enda was careful and cautious. Neither of them had their mother's nervous nature. She was a small, sharp-boned woman whose blonde hair had started to thin early. Mrs. Kelly who caught Dick taking her clothes off the line, and was told that it would only cost 50 pence extra if she wanted them folded, and Mrs. McGregor, who answered the door to Dick selling flowers he'd picked from her own garden, believed he was the cause of his mother's hair loss, and they weren't the only ones.

From the age of six, Dick had the women in the estate harassed.

"Can you not just play like any other boy?" Mrs. Hurley begged after a visit from Mrs. Kelly, who lived in the pristine white bungalow near the entrance of the estate. As a child, she'd grown up surrounded by green fields but the space had grown smaller and smaller each year. She did not look kindly on the residents of the estate. She was a thick girted woman with a tint of pink in her curled hair and a jaw of loose flesh. Her dark eyes were small and mean. That Dick would choose her house showed a cluelessness that worried his mother. Enda apparently had stayed by the iron gates. He would have watched his brother pulling the clothes from the line.

"Did you try to stop him?" she asked, and he shook his head. She could imagine him hiding behind the walls when he heard Mrs. Kelly calling out from the kitchen. It was hard to know what Enda was thinking, if he was following his brother blindly, or if he had a hand in his brothers' doings, though she suspected the former.

The boys never went near Mrs. Kelly again and for the most part their neighbors found them entertaining and cute. If they didn't they were quick to tell the boys to get lost and stop banging on their doors. No one found a need to complain to Mrs. Hurley and worry her. When the boys went on strike outside Bertie Rawles house she didn't hear about it for days. Then it was told to her by her husband who'd gone for his weekly pint in the Dun Maeve. He was a tall, excruciatingly thin man with an untidy mop of dark hair. The last time she accompanied him to the bar; some-one had the gall to say, "Jaysus is she not feeding ya?"

She felt sick with shame for herself and Tadgh. But even without the insult she probably wouldn't have gone back. She couldn't relax when she was away from her boys. She still dreamed of Dick running away from her and having to leave Enda behind. It seemed the experience had gotten worse as time went by. While she was living it, she thought of nothing but catching Dick. But in the years since there were thoughts of her son floating in the river or running straight out onto the road or Enda turning and going towards the quarry and further still to the marshes and rocks of the bay and she'd feel her heart going a hundred miles an hour and her chest tighten.

"Wait until you hear," Tadgh said.

They were in the living room. The last embers of the fire were going out. She hated the sour smell of drink and was glad when he stood by the fire place with his coat still on from the excitement. "The boys were doing deliveries."

She told him she knew. A cold feeling had started in her neck. She should be proud of her boys coming up with these ideas and plans but she was a woman who would have preferred anonymity.

"Well, do you know about Bertie?" he said and waited for her to say no before saying, "They did a delivery for him and he refused to pay their 50 pence. He said they needed to know how to run a business and when a man wants his fags he shouldn't be kept waiting."

"He got them to buy fags?"

Her husband waved her protest away.

"So, they sat in his garden. Hilary Sands next door said it must have been two hours they were there."

"I'm sure she was looking out her window the whole time."

Tadgh frowned. He didn't like to talk badly of anyone. Dick had gotten that off him, this innocent belief that everyone was alright, which led him to people like Mrs. Kelly who still clicked her tongue when she saw them at mass.

"No," she spotted them around 10.30 and wouldn't have thought of them again if she hadn't heard the shouts. It was lunch time at the quarry."

Tadgh started laughing and his wife couldn't help smile. Bertie Rawles was not a man known for his generosity or fondness towards kids. The two boys would have looked out of place in his garden.

"What are you doing there?" the men might have asked, "Waiting for ole Bert to die."

"Nigel Hession and Sam Brady and Frank McGuire were at the gate shouting at Bertie to pay the boys. Come on give them their fifty pence."

Mrs. Hurley covered her mouth and laughed.

"There was a bit of a crowd by the time Bertie was drawn

out of his hole. He comes out with his fifty pence and our boys tell him they aren't moving for anything less than a pound. 'Time is money,' Dick says, and the men are howling in laughter telling Bertie to go on and get the notes from under his mattress." Tadgh paused to catch his breath and said, "If they can get a pound out of Bertie Rawles, they can do anything."

Mrs. Hurley wasn't so sure. If Bertie Rawles didn't live in the bungalows near the quarry the boys could have been sitting there for days without getting their money. Dick was impulsive with his ideas and she worried that Enda didn't think for himself.

"Still the boys are lucky they have each other."

Enda couldn't count the amount of times he'd heard his mother saying that. There was always an air of wistfulness in her voice that he found strange, since she'd grown up in a house with five girls. It would be years later and Dick would be gone before she'd explain that she was the youngest out of the whole gang of them. Eight years separated her from Tessa. The eldest three were either married or working in the town by the time she was seven and Tessa never had much interest.

"So that's why I had the two of ye so close together. It's sad the way things turn out."

Enda would be in his twenties at that stage. He'd put his hand on his mother's and smile, but he couldn't say it was okay. He and his brother had had plans.

As early as fifteen and fourteen they'd decided they would seek their fortunes elsewhere.

The family had just finished grace when Enda first told his parents, "We're going to London."

"Can you wait till after dinner?" The father said and everyone but the mother laughed. That evening at the table with her hands poised after blessing herself, she had the look of an injured bird. "What will you do?" she asked.

"We'll take the tube to Kilburn, then the 16 bus to Cricklewood," Dick said. Their father chuckled and their mother said that's not funny.

"There's money over there," Enda said, "Michael Raines is making three hundred a week."

"He's an electrician, and it was still hard for him to get work," their mother said.

"It was not."

Their mother was surprised and hurt by Dick's argument. It took a moment before she said, "Yes it most certainly was. Ester was very worried for a while."

"Well it doesn't matter, we're going," Enda said.

"Can you please say something?" she said to her husband, a barber who came home with not much more than a hundred pounds a week and had unbeknownst to anyone started to die. He shrugged and said that if his boys were determined there was nothing he could do to stop them, but they had to finish school first. The boys didn't have much interest in school. Dick studied business but he preferred to be out selling door to door, instead of reading about it from books. Enda loved woodworking and would often stay late to finish a piece, but he didn't see how a leaving cert would make any difference to him.

"Math is about angles too, you need to know these things," their father insisted. "And there's more to business than coming up with ideas."

"We know that," Dick said. "But we don't need to learn that in the classroom. We need to go to London."

The father smirked and said, "To the buildings." He found the idea of Dick on the sites comical with his thin waist and narrow shoulders. Dick had never liked anything physical, not even Gaelic football. The humor in his father's face didn't bother Dick. He was immune to people's reactions to the point of being ignorant. Enda had seen the usefulness in it. His indifference made him thick skinned. Dick was the perfect man to knock on doors and ask for money without a bit of doubt in his voice. At sixteen, he'd gone to different shops around Sligo town and asked for permission to put their names in a book of brochures, giving a 10% discount for products or service.

"You know how it works, you charge a higher price and don't lose any money," he told one mechanic on High Street. The mechanic said Dick should be a politician and then, "Go on, put me down."

There was a florist, two bakers, three mechanics, a hairdresser, a clothes shop, two fast food restaurants, a furniture store and printing service. The book a flimsy production of pale blue cost five pounds.

"It's a brilliant idea," Dick told Enda, "Everyone wants to save money."

In their estate, Enda and Dick went together to the doors. To go separate would have everyone asking 'Where's Dick?' or

'Where's Enda?' and it would be tiresome and time consuming. Bertie Rawles who was in his seventies told them to fuck off. Ester Raines, large and middle-aged, sighed and asked what she would do with that since she was never in town, but she bought one anyway. Mrs. Kelly's son who had taken over the house after her death and looked like her, bar the pink tinted hair and scowl said he expected to be reading about the boys in Forbes someday. In the space of a week, with forty houses, they made 60 pounds.

Sligo was different. They had decided to go to each house solo to save time. Enda lasted two houses and refused to do any more. He didn't like the worry he saw on the people's faces and found it hard to speak from nerves. But he kept Dick company for a week while he hit the estates from Cranmore to Cartron. During that time, Dick sold five books.

"There's no money here," Dick said to his father later. "We need to go."

"Yeah, I've heard, to the buildings," his father smiled.

"What's so funny?" Enda said.

"Nothing," their father could keep a straight face when he looked at his youngest son with his broad shoulders and large hands. Enda had been a Gaelic footballer in his early teens. He'd been good too, until he'd gotten distracted by the girls. Nora Parkes wasn't the first to turn his head, but she was the first serious girlfriend. A year older with a slim body and daring blue eyes, he'd spent his fifteenth summer in her house and taking walks with her to the old graveyard. He never talked about his exploits, though it was obvious that something was going on. He'd become quiet and insular and tended to move through the house at all hours. More than once there were red and purple bruises on his neck.

"I don't know what's wrong with you young people," his mother cried when she saw them. "You're like animals."

"Those are love bites, Mam," Dick said with a grin.

"I don't care what they're called."

During the Nora Parke summer, Dick missed his brother but said nothing. When Enda came bursting into the house one afternoon and locked himself in the room to listen to 'Thin Lizzy' full volume, Dick did a little jig in the kitchen until his mother appeared at the door and asked, "What in heavens name is going on?"

Enda never said why they split up, though Dick suspected Nora had gotten herself a new interest. The brothers were fifteen and sixteen, and it was the year their father's health faded. Early October their mother met the boys after school and told them that their father had fainted at work. In the hospital, they sat in the waiting room with the white walls and soft chairs. Their mother cried quietly. Enda sat slumped beside her. "Can you sit down?" he asked Dick.

"No, I can't," Dick said. His school uniform looked wrong on his thin figure. His face was narrow and his dark hair cut neatly. The trousers were too short on the legs; he looked like a man pretending and failing to be a boy. There was seriousness in him that Enda had always trusted. At this stage he viewed his brother as the most honest person he knew because there was no hiding or pretending with Dick. Even in the Sligo General with their mother's tears and the clatter of footsteps and their father lying prone in some room, he could not hide the fear that this would put a dent in their plans. He only had to look at Enda and Enda could see the question in his eyes. Enda nodded and said, "It'll be fine."

His mother found his hand and sobbed.

"There's no stopping the Hurleys," Dick said when they were told that their father was going to be okay.

The doctor said, "He'll be fine if he does what I tell him. He has to take seven injections a day."

Mrs. Hurley nodded and the doctor took the seat beside her. She was like a child, though in actual fact she was older than any of her neighbors assumed. Her hair had started to thin well into her forties and she was nearly sixty when she was told that her husband had diabetes. The boys felt victorious that night. To take seven shots a day and finish their leaving certificate seemed simple. While their mother lay curled up on the chair in her husband's hospital room, they celebrated on the basketball courts behind the school. Empty beer cans were scattered around the feet of the huddled teenage figures. There was the usual gang, the Hurleys, Faith Wheeler, Breen Timmons, Martha Tills and Matthew Daly. Nora joined them late in the evening when lights in the housing estates had started to turn off and the silence was like a bubble surrounding the village. She was holding Stan Hession's hand. He was an untidy, wide shouldered, tall boy, whose body was on the verge of fat. His hair fell over his eyes and he seemed to be enjoying the tension his presence caused.

"So what are we doing?"Nora asked, and sat beside skinny Martha.

"Truth or Dare," Martha said and handed her the joint.

"It's your turn," Enda said.

They waited for Nora to smoke. She might have had her eyes on Enda all the time, though it was hard to tell. Smoke rose towards the moonlight and she said, "Alright."

"What is it then?"

"Truth," she said and passed the joint to Stan. "Don't mind if I do," he said.

Enda asked, "Were you shifting that wanker during the summer?"

Stan spluttered and said, "Watch it Hurley."

There was a pause where all eyes were on Nora. Maybe the girls knew the answer already.

"No," she said.

Stan laughed and said, "Tell the truth."

Enda was on his feet like a shot. Stan was up after him, and Nora was telling him to sit down for God sake.

"Grow up," Faith Wheeler said, "Stop acting like eejit's."

Martha Tills was on her feet, shouting that it was her bloody turn and "I dare Dick to take a swim."

"Don't be stupid," Enda said. Dick had been sitting with his legs crossed and his arms over them. His head was tilted to the side. He'd been quiet for ages, enthralled with the river that sounded so furious.

"Do you hear that?" was the last thing he'd said. "The river's alive." And he'd gotten a shove from someone and been told to stop talking shite.

Now, Dick said, "Okay so," and stood.

His brother told him to sit right back down. A stone wall separated the courts from the river. The night lights barely made it that far, though the rush of water had been a sound track to the kids playing ball and cracking beers open. If Dick went to that wall, his brother wouldn't move. He'd watch and probably know that Dick had no intention of jumping, and all the while big thick Stan Hession would be waiting.

The bridge would be different. He would have to run through the school grounds and passed Toolan's shop and the waste of green to the railings, and that would be the end of the strain between the boys.

Enda said, "You're not jumping in there."

Dick said, "That's true." There was a strange feeling around them as if someone had pierced a hole in the night and the air was seeping out. Everyone was afraid to look at Enda and Stan.

Dick shouted, "The bridge," and started to run. Enda was shouting behind him but Dick was fast. He felt light and as quick as a bird with the others running after him, shouting and cursing. Maybe he would jump from the bridge. It was just an eight foot drop. The water was high. There'd be no chance of hitting a rock and the water would be cool and refreshing. He was hot now. The school was dead quiet. The shop was closed and his shoes slapping the pavement brought a rhythm into his head. He whooped. Enda had never been as fast; no one had.

Dick saw the bridge ahead and on the other side of the street was the statue of Our Lady with her arms raised towards the sky. Dick was tempted to run over to her and say 'look at me' like he used to as a boy. He'd often been seen jumping up and down, to try and get in her line of sight while his brother laughed. It had upset Dick that the statue was always gazing upward. When he'd asked his mother why Our Lady never looked at him, his mother said, "Ah she's watching you alright, only you don't know it."

His mother was convinced that he'd been running to the statue when he was three. He'd wanted to catch our Lady by surprise. "Boo," he would have said.

But he didn't have time for that nonsense now. His brother was close. The lights from the Dun Maeve reflected off the black water. He ran to the middle of the bridge and the rails were higher than he thought. He couldn't get his leg over at first and was steadying himself in a straddle when his brother was beside him, panting and red-faced. If he tried to pull Dick down, he risked the chance of pushing him in. The others were around him, breathless and huddled, as if Dick was something to fear. He glanced at the water below and Enda said, "You do that and fuck London, I swear to God."

"He's not going anywhere, are you Dick?" Nora said and wee Faith in her army coat told her to shut up. The water was tempting as Dick imagined the handle of the kitchen door had been when he was three.

"I'm telling you," Enda said, "You do this and I'm done."

Enda's face was clear in the street light. He might have been stoned and drunk but his stare was focused and his anger firm. He meant what he said. Dick could hear his breathing and felt the heat in his chest. All he'd have to do was slip to the side but he would be slipping away from his brother. He could feel it already. Their fragile bond was a thin white thread and made him lean towards the ground.

Afterwards, he'd wish he'd gone over the bridge. He'd imagine the splash of the water and how his coat would have spread around him and dragged him away from the screaming kids. Enda would have been the loudest. He would have cursed and sworn, and it wouldn't have mattered. Because what they didn't know that night, as Dick slipped back to the pavement with a renewed heaviness, was that he would be going alone anyway.

That year, Nora got pregnant and Dick passed his leaving cert exams. He got a job in the local garage while he waited for Enda. At the back of the house under his mother's terrified eyes, he burnt his uniform.

Their father lay in the living room. He hadn't been at work in the barber shop for weeks. "Have you taken all your injections?" was a daily refrain from the mother but she couldn't give them to him. She couldn't face the sight of the needle piercing her husband's skin. Maybe things would have been different if she had been stronger, though it was possible that his diabetes had gone unchecked too long to matter. His fatal heart attack came the November of Enda's final year at school.

Months of silence followed. Dick worked the night shift in the garage, which meant he was home for their mother when Enda went to school. A woman who had spent all her time running around her house in a nervous frizzy, she started to spend the day in bed or curled up on the couch. Sometimes Dick and

Enda would put on the television but she never seemed to watch it. Neighbors came to see her. Ester and Maggie and Mrs. Parkes, but the quiet would be dense with their presence and the boys hated the pity on the visitor's face. They never stayed long, a cup of tea and they were standing. They were inclined to whisper when they told Dick or Enda that they were close by if the boys needed them.

On a fine March morning, Mrs. Hurley left her home in the Woodland housing estate and walked past her neighbors' houses, the small green, and Lavin Construction, to turn left onto the main road. Luckily the secondary school was not at recess so no student saw her wandering in her nightdress and slippers. Annette Lenihan, working in the shop beside the school, noticed the figure in white passing the window. No one knew where Mrs. Hurley had been headed. She would not say when Annette stopped her at the bridge or when the doctor asked in the hospital. The boys reacted to her hospitalization in different ways. Dick became quieter and pensive. He could sit for hours at the kitchen table, alone with his thoughts. While Enda was restless, his jaws constantly tight, and his body tense. The simplest thing could set him off.

Scalding beans made him throw his spoon onto the table and curse. They were having their tea with the picture of the Sacred Heart looking down at them. Any time Enda glanced at it, he wanted to tear it off the wall. Dick refused to look at the image. He had a strange sensation that it was his heart left out in the open. It stung to be sitting at their table and not be able to speak about their future. They were stuck in this house and town. Dick was despondent, but his brother's anger surprised him. Enda had always been quiet about London and Dick had often worried that Enda had been humoring him. Enda got up from the table without finishing his tea and stood at the back door. The garden was untidy with long grass and plants their mother had started to tend before their father died.

"We need to do something," Enda said.

Dick pushed his plate away. A bean had fallen onto his pants and left a trail of orange but he couldn't care less. "Like what?"

"I don't know," Enda said, "Something." He was still in his uniform with the frayed sleeved sweater. His face was tight as he watched his brother light up a cigarette. Enda had never been one to smoke. If their mother was here, Dick would have had to go outside. As it was he used his plate as an ashtray.

"Are you working tonight?" Enda asked and was told of course. Dick worked seven nights a week in the garage down the road. It was easier than spending time in the house. Enda often went to his brother. Unable to sleep and bored at home with RTÉ going off at 11pm, he'd wander down to play cards or sneak into the lot with the used cars. Recently there was a surge of second hand cars bought and the boss had to leave a few at front. Their keys were kept in the main office. The other night, with the rain pattering against the glass of the kiosk and drowning out the radio, Dick said that he needed to use the bathroom before Pat locked up, and he'd noticed how easy it would have been to grab a set of keys to one of the cars out front.

Dick wished he hadn't told Enda. He could see his brother thought too much about it. He'd been like that in Bertie Rawle's garden. Enda was quiet and serious faced before he surprised everyone by saying he wanted a pound, and with Nora Parkes too. The night they were playing spin the bottle and he picked up the bottle and put it down facing Nora, his expression was so grave and confident no one thought of arguing with him. Nora gushed and stood and the two never came back for the rest of the night.

In the kitchen with the old photos that had gotten hard to glance at, Enda looked like a caged animal. And the more Enda looked trapped the more Dick worried that Enda might be the first to take off. Dick hadn't spoken about leaving for weeks now, but he dreamed about it every day. The idea of abandoning his brother was like a noose around his neck. Every time he considered it he felt it tighten from the guilt, which made him think of it more. Most afternoons he thought of getting the bus to Holyhead and the Ferry from there. No one would notice until his shift started. His boss would probably phone the house. He'd be raging, asking "Where's your bloody brother?" Enda would say he's not his brother's keeper, but he might offer to go down and work. Then he'd have the job and something to do in the evenings. He'd always said he'd like a few pounds of his own and to get out of the house at night. Enda would be walking to the garage and Dick would be halfway to London.

"Can you get the keys for the Golf?" Enda said. He was smiling now. He looked close to happy and Dick had an urge to say, "What if I go ahead to London and you follow? There's no point in the two of us waiting around?"

"Tonight," Dick said instead and Enda said, "Fuck yeah, let's take it out for a ride. No one is ever about. We could take it to Strandhill or the Coolaney road."

Dick put out his cigarette and wiped the bean sauce on his trousers.

"Come on Dick, I have to do something."

"Right," Dick said, "But not till after 2."

Enda got down to Dick around 11. They played poker and gin rummy and Enda was smiling in a way he hadn't done in months. Dick watched his younger brother. With his blue eyes and strong jaw Enda was handsome in a way Dick would never be. Dick was too skinny and long in the face to ever be deemed good looking. Enda wouldn't find it hard to get some woman for company and if he didn't get the job in the garage, at least he had his wood-work. He'd started to stay later and later in the workshop. He could do a carpentry course, and that would benefit any business they might start. Dick could send money to help him and their mother. He'd start researching all the options and have it ready to set up, but of course he'd wait for Enda before he started their business. They were young yet, 19 and 18, they could take their time. It all seemed perfect until he thought of their mother, pale and foreign in the hospital, and the hardship of having her at home, when to leave her to go to the shops weighed on you.

The night had a stillness like held breathe. Stars were blocked by the trees at the front of the garage. Beyond them were blackened fields and behind the garage was the river. Dick could hear it when he stepped out of the kiosk. The radio had been turned off and he wished it hadn't been. The dense quiet had the feel of disaster coming. Enda was at the car and clinging to the passenger door handle, impatient to get going. His restlessness was constant now, brought by the silence in his house that went on and on. It had been decided earlier that Dick would be the first to drive and Enda would take the journey home. But Dick was taking his time and Enda realized his brother was scared. He was probably hoping Enda would pull him back like the time he was about to jump the bridge. It never occurred to Enda until now that Dick had accepted the dare because he had been banking on Enda to stop him.

Enda had no compulsion to turn away from the car though. His pulse had quickened and he felt an excitement like the kind he'd experienced when his hand slid between Nora Parkes' legs.

The brothers had talked about taking the corners in Coolaney and seeing the sheer mountain drop while doing sixty. They'd said that once they started they might not be able to stop and they'd be all the way to Cork by the time anyone woke up. But Dick wasn't able to put the key in the door. He might have paled. It was hard to see in the dim lights. His voice was low when he said they were taking too much of a chance. They might want green cards in the future and couldn't have a bad record. Enda's disappointment took up space inside him. He felt heavy and tired from it.

"You're all talk," Enda said.

Over the roof of the car, Dick said, "I can't stay."

"Well get into the fucking car then."

"No, I mean here, in this town."

Enda's hand fell, "Who says you should be the one who gets to leave?"

Dick felt an icy fear when his brother said, "Let's toss for it."

Dick watched his brother step back from the car and wander towards him with the fifty pence coin in his hand. The brothers stood facing each other, dark and fair, one scared, the other angry, and Enda gave him the choice.

He said, "What will it be Dick?"

In the hospital, their mother reedy and doll-like with stringy hair and startled blue eyes, told Dick, "You can't go off without him."

"What choice do I have?"

"You can start something here."

"There's no bloody money here."

"Don't curse," her gaze shifted to her youngest son. "Enda," she said.

He shrugged, and said, "It's alright Mam."

"But will you go too?" she said, and the air was pulled from the room. Dick's anger towards his mother surprised him. They'd always been careful not to upset her but he wanted to grab her bony arms and say of course Enda's coming.

Michael Raines had gotten Dick a job brick-laying and he'd sort Enda out too.

"Enda," his mother said.

Dick hadn't noticed the quiet, but it had made their mother slump on the bed.

"Enda reached for her hand and said, "It'll be alright."

But it wasn't alright. Their mother was kept in hospital for weeks and when she got out she refused to leave the house. Dick phoned from London every Sunday.

"When can you come?" Dick would ask and Enda would look at his mother beside him and say, "Not yet. I can't yet."

His words were clipped with anger, while Dick wanted to cry. London was not how Dick had imagined, though it was hard to remember what he thought it would be. Certainly not so grey and busy. There was a flatness to it that made him feel he was on the outside looking in. He could stand in the middle of the sidewalk and people would weave around his body without glancing at him. Dick didn't see Michael Raines except for the occasional glance at the pub. Michael had brought him to the hostel and given him directions to the site. Six years older and never friends, he'd done his bit.

The room Dick shared with three other men stank of sweat and feet, and six mornings a week Dick was up at 5am to travel to buildings sites. During his Sunday phone calls home, he said nothing to Enda about the leaking toilet in the hostel, the pain in his back that had not left after his third day, or the 29 pounds he earned for a ten hour day which meant he could never afford an apartment alone. He didn't mention the Crown pub either, where he had a pint waiting for him. In the phone box, the daylight would hurt his eyes and he'd tap his feet to the music coming from the pub. Dick spent his spare time drinking among burly Irish lads with wide backs and calloused hands.

They liked to nudge him and say, "So what's it this week?"

He'd raise his glass and tell them, "Plants for office buildings, bringing color to life." And someone would clink his glass and say, "To plants."

There would be laughter. They might have been taking the mickey, but on the barstool Dick never cared.

"Paving," he said to his brother one week, "We could do commercial and residential."

"What about the landscaping service?"

"I'm not giving up on that one. We need to keep our minds open and the paving would be more money. Then we could go into other stuff. What do you think?"

"Yeah, it sounds good. Are you alright over there, Dick?"

"I'll be better when you're here."

Dick didn't go home the first Christmas and by the second there had been no change. On the bus ride from Dublin to Sligo with the early morning mist settling on the window, the quiet stillness of the grey winter fields made Dick feel a life-time had passed since he'd left.

With her tired eyes and pale skin, their mother had aged significantly in two years. Dick sat at the kitchen table with her. His head hurt from the pub the night before and the tea gave him heartburn, but he tried to hide the discomfort. His mother was swallowed up in her woolen jumper. She hadn't gotten any easier to talk to and Enda had been reluctant to pressure her during the holidays. He was out now so Dick said, "It's going good over there, Mam. I have a few ideas for when Enda comes over."

His mother nodded and said, "But there's no rush, is there Dick?"

Dick's hand tightened on the mug. He had an urge to fling it and imagined her fright. "We're not getting any younger," Dick said and his mother smiled weakly and said, "Neither am I."

He drank the tea and the discomfort from the heartburn was a blessing. It took from the frustration. He would have liked to say that she was being selfish, that the time was slipping from them already. He was twenty-three for God sake but he nodded and let her talk about the senior citizens meetings she started go to on a Wednesday with her friend Ester.

To Enda, he asked if Ester could watch their mother. She visited their mother most days anyway. "What about nights?" Enda said.

"She sleeps," Dick said.

Enda told him he was an awful eejit and it was too much to ask anyone.

"Alright," Dick said, "We wait."

Dick continued to phone on Sunday. His mother always answered. She'd ask how he was. Sometimes she'd enquire if there was anyone special. Women made Dick nervous, but he only tutted and said he had no time for that nonsense. Their mother didn't like to talk about herself.

"How are you Mam?" would lead to a pause only for her to sigh and say, "You know me."

He would know then that there was no difference and his conversation with Enda would be strained. He could imagine his mother standing beside Enda when she handed the phone to him, listening to everything he said with those worried eyes. Enda's form would be reflected in the oval mirror on the hall wall. His head would be down and his shoulders hunched. Over the years, Enda had filled out to become a broad, languorous man.

He'd gotten quiet and morose and the Christmas visits became tougher, because there was nothing Dick could do to ease him. He wanted Enda to visit him in London, but Enda said that was impossible with the mother too nervous to travel. All they had was their few days at Christmas and the phone calls. When the mother told him one Sunday about the moving statue of Ballinspittle and the pilgrims that were flocking there, Dick thought of the statue of Our Lady in the town never glancing at them and said to his brother, "Maybe we should do the trek to Cork and pray to that one for an answer."

"If I thought it would do any good, I might," Enda said.

Dick was twenty-six, and he felt old the year his mother was sent to the hospital due to blurred vision and numbness in her arms. They were told that she'd had a series of mini strokes. The next Christmas was harder. Their mother was quieter and more anxious than usual, and Enda was fiery and restless. Christmas Eve, he asked Dick if he could have one night without getting rat-arsed drunk.

"It's fucking Christmas," Dick said

Enda said, "It's Christmas all the time for you."

Dick understood his anger from being stuck at home all these years, working in a struggling furniture shop four miles away and having to come back to his mother. Dick would have gone insane if it had been him. After three days at home, he was ready to jump on the bus. He'd return to London, only to start the wait for his brother's phone call. Every evening, at the hostel where he paid extra for a private room; he'd ask if there were any messages from home and feel a stab of hope, tiny compared to when he first arrived, but there nonetheless.

The April of his seventh year, the landlady, a large bosomed woman in her sixties, smiled and finally said, "Your brother called."

Dick whooped and clapped his hands and said, "Today's the fucking day."

He was told to watch his mouth.

Enda answered the phone. "When will you be here?" Dick said, and the silence stretched. Later, he'd think he should have known the moment his mother failed to greet him.

Dick flew home for the funeral, but it was hard to stay in his mother's house. Her scent of lavender and soap lingered in every room and the place was burdened with her belongings. He could hardly bring his head up to look at them. From the kitchen table, he gestured to the Sacred Heart, "What will you do with that?"

Enda was standing by the sink. The top buttons of his shirt was open and his tie loose.

"She never said. Wouldn't you think she'd have said?" Enda answered.

"She knew you were leaving," Dick said.

Enda shrugged and told him it was hard to know what she knew.

"She wasn't deaf," Dick said.

Enda said it depended on what was being said.

The whiskey bottle was empty, but still Dick picked it up and turned it upside down as if something might emerge. The back door was open, letting in cool air.

After a while he said, "Porches, they're the way to go nowadays, a two man job. I've been looking around. People pay 300 pounds at least and we could build one in a day, maybe less. We could do seven days a week and then we'd cut it down to five. Within a couple of years we could have people working for us."

Enda took the seat beside him. "What about transport and material?" he said, "There's a lot of cost when starting out."

Dick felt a quickening in his chest. He leaned forward, his mother's things forgotten for now.

He said, "I've been researching and it's doable."

Enda nodded. He seemed distracted all of a sudden, and Dick wondered if he was thinking of all those other ventures they'd had to let go, like the aluminum windows Dick could have gotten for cheap, the stonework partnership, and the landscape business they'd wanted to buy. His brother was gazing out the back door. It had started to get dark but still there was the sound of children at play. Eventually he said. "I can't sell the sacred heart."

"Who cares about the Sacred Heart?"

Enda frowned at him, and Dick said, "Okay, bring it with you then."

"Fine, I will," Enda said and Dick didn't know if it was a joke or not.

It was decided Enda would stay to take care of the house while Dick went back to work. The house was in a worse state than they thought. The whole place had to be painted. The attic and windows needed insulation. A shower needed to be put in, and all this, while Dick was getting impatient. He'd gotten his brother a job on the sites and was anxious to get out of the cramped hostel and into their own place. A month rolled into three.

When Enda answered the phone and said, "There's something I need to tell you," Dick had to close his eyes from the exasperation.

Behind him, music spilled out from the pub and there was the low hum of traffic, but all sound vanished when Enda said, "I met a woman. She's a friend of Maurice Lavin's."

"What are you doing with that eejit?"

Enda said Maurice wasn't so bad. He'd helped get the house ready to sell and he'd given him a job in the quarry for the last weeks. Dick waited. The pause was loaded. "Her name's Eilish," Enda said.

Dick said he couldn't care less what her name was. "When are you coming over?" he asked.

Enda said. "The thing is she's pregnant."

Dick said, "You're joking?"

And his brother told him he was totally serious. Dick was starting to feel claustrophobic and had to put his hand on the glass to settle himself. He didn't know how his brother could be so stupid.

'You should know,' she says, as if she'd just run into the car. Then she says she's having my baby. I'm expecting her to start bawling but she doesn't. She stands to leave and she would have gone if I hadn't called her."

"Oh," Dick said.

His mouth had gone dry and he didn't want to know anything more about Eilish, but his brother had grown silent and he was forced to ask what they were going to do.

His brother said, "We're getting married."

"Ah for feck sake," Dick said.

"I'm sorry," Enda said, "Some things you can't plan for."

Dick said, "Eight years."

There was nothing his brother could say to that.

Dick said, "For feck sake," and hung up.

Dick's hand dropped from the phone. He might have been standing there hours. He didn't know. His mouth was dry and he felt immune to the sounds around him. The inside of the pub was dark. A few of the lads from work were there. A lad from Cork nursing his beer at the counter asked if he was okay. Dick nodded. He didn't have the will to explain. He finished his pint and asked for another. For days, Dick was ripped of energy. It wasn't anger he felt. Anger would have been better than the crippling disappointment that made every act a chore.

The next week when he phoned home a woman answered and said hello. He hung up. He wasn't about to chat with Eilish and pretend everything was alright. He hated Eilish and her "I suppose you should know." He imagined her perched on his mother's couch. She would have had her hands tucked between her legs and her head down and she would have looked at his brother with watery puppy dog eyes. He thought his brother was a fool. He'd fallen for the oldest trick in the book. Their mother was hardly cold in the grave and already the woman had honed in and now Dick didn't have their weekly phone call to look forward to. The last time they talked, Enda seemed strained and Dick imagined the woman standing in the hall with her arms crossed. She was probably afraid Enda would say something about her or that Dick would ask, "Enda, come on, tell the truth, how are you?"

Then Enda would tell him that it was awful. Just when he was freed of one responsibility another had risen. In the meantime, Dick had wasted years waiting. He'd been putting everything off and so many businesses had gone through his fingers. When he'd arrived in the country he was young, now his back hurt and his hands were rough. And every now and again that woman would answer the phone in his mother's home and he'd get so angry he'd want to put the phone through the glass.

A few Sundays after he'd first heard Eilish's name, Enda told him, "We've set a date."

Dick didn't have a clue what he was talking about until Enda added, "It's in a couple of weeks. Eilish doesn't want to be too big on the day."

"Well she should have thought of that," Dick said.

Enda said, "Will you come?"

He might have said no, if he didn't think there was a chance of saving his brother yet.

Dick got the bus from Dublin airport and sat in the back. It was raining. The green fields glistened and Dick watched the drops slide down the window. Eilish had moved into the mother's home days before. Enda said it had been his idea. There was no point in her renting an apartment. "It keeps me out of trouble," he said, and Dick thought she is the trouble.

He was the only one to get off at the village. He alighted outside Sheridan's butchers amid a gaggle of kids in navy school uniforms. The street wasn't busy like it used to be. In the years of his absence, the village had been bypassed. From certain areas he could see the traffic on the motorway and it felt like he'd fallen back into a hole. The supermarket across the way was quiet. He saw a tiny lady in a scarf come out and no one else. Faith Wheeler's café at the top of the street was open. She did great sandwiches, but Dick didn't feel like sitting in there now. He went the other way. He passed the fast food restaurant and strolled towards the river. Across the bridge he would have turned left, and left again after the school for his mother's house, but the Dun Maeve pub was impossible to pass.

The bar was cozy with low tables down the center of the floor, and red lounge couches around the edges of the room. The girl behind the bar was young with dark sullen eyes and a slow walk. He ordered a pint of Guinness and had a few gulps before phoning his brother. Eilish answered and he had to resist the temptation to hang up.

"Hello," she said. Her voice was low and sure. He imagined her sitting on the hall table with her legs crossed.

"Is Enda there?" Dick asked, and she countered with who is this, as if she didn't know.

"His brother, is he there?"

"No."

Dick sighed, and said, "Will you tell him I'm in the Dun Maeve? I'll wait for him here."

Dick sat at the bar and ordered another pint. He had a one-sided conversation with the bar-girl. He told her that he'd come back for his brother's wedding. It would be a small affair with the bride and groom, Maurice Lavin and his wife Ann, as well as himself. He told the girl that he knew nothing about the bride. Apparently, she didn't have a family, but how did they know if that was true. The family might have disowned her. For all he knew, she could be a psychopath or one of those women who seduced men and took everything they had. She could have husbands dotted around the country. The only thing to vouch for her was she was Maurice Lavin's friend and that didn't say much, since Maurice Lavin was a bollix.

He drank and asked, "Do you know Maurice?" The bargirl shrugged and said her mother worked for him.

"Doesn't everyone?" he said. The bar-girl was standing against the back of the bar with her arms crossed. She was watching him with what seemed like suspicion. Her attention made him uncomfortable and he wished his brother was there to take the high stool beside him. It was after 5.30 when Dick ordered his third pint. His brother should be home by now. Maybe the wife-to-be hadn't given him the message. His brother was saying I wonder where Dick is and she was studying her nails and telling him she had no idea.

Nigel Downs was at the other end of the bar talking to himself. Some people who might have been staying in the rooms upstairs were at the tables by the fire, eating dinner. There was no one else but the bar-girl to talk to. She should lose some weight, Dick thought. He said there was no best man thank God. He'd dreaded having to write a speech. What could he say? Congratulations on the quickest pregnancy ever?

He said, "She didn't waste any time and now she's sitting in my parent's house and I feel like I'm intruding."

"That's not fair," the girl said, "they can't take the house."

He was surprised she was listening. He shrugged and said, "They're buying my half from me."

She nodded and said oh, and he wished he hadn't told her that so quickly. Her interest had fled. He could have told her that Enda wasn't giving him what the house was worth. He was giving half of what their parents agreed to thirty years ago. He drank deeply and was wiping his chin when the door opened to his brother. Enda said, "Hey, welcome home."

Dick said, "It's about bloody time." He saw the woman behind his brother, but thought she was someone passing through. She was probably looking for a room because she was glancing around the bar, as if it was her first time to see it, when his brother hugged him. When Dick was released, the woman was standing too close to them, and though she was smiling she was looking at Dick with an interest he found disturbing.

"This is Eilish," Enda said, and Dick was sure the bar-girl smiled. Eilish was not what he'd expected. There was nothing demure or soft about her. She was nearly as tall as his brother and though she was slender, she had swimmer's shoulders. Her dark hair was long and tied back. Her eyes were the color of granite. Dick's head felt sore all of a sudden. He hadn't considered she wouldn't let Enda out alone. He'd imagined he and Enda would sit at the bar and get drunk and talk about the mess Enda had gotten himself into. But here she was, saying that it was nice to meet him, and Dick said it was nice to meet her too, when all he wanted was to tell her to feck off.

"Do you want to grab a table?" Enda said. Eilish said sure and went towards the back of the pub. Enda ordered a couple of pints and an orange juice. Dick ordered a couple of whiskies

"Not for me," Enda said.

Dick said, "Ah go on, have a shot," and nodded at the bargirl who seemed to have perked up. She moved quickly to get the whiskey, and Dick thought she wasn't so bad. Enda pushed the glass away.

"So," Dick said, after he'd downed both shots, "That's her," and Enda said. "Yes, it is."

Enda sat beside Eilish on the lounge seat. Dick took the low stool opposite them. He couldn't believe it when her hand went to the inside of his brother's thigh; the gesture of ownership was worse than her long drawn out hellos on the phone. She was talking about the wedding and how she wouldn't have been able to stand the attention of a big ceremony. Besides, she said, there was hardly any point with their parents gone. Her voice didn't hold any of the high pitched excitement Dick assumed women would have when talking about their weddings. She was matter of fact, maybe even a little bored, and she was too preoccupied with his pint. Every time he took a drink she kept her gaze on the glass. He didn't want to imagine what she'd be like at home.

Enda asked if Dick had done anything about the porches. Dick had gone to a couple of banks for a loan. The first manager breezed through the paperwork, before sliding the folder across the table and telling him that there was nothing there to convince him. Dick had no assets and no training to make him stand out out from the crowd. The second manager asked what experience he had running a business and ignored the paperwork. Dick would have to work for at least another five years on the buildings to save enough money, but he didn't say that.

He said, "Absolutely, plans are in action."

Then he stood, and said more pints, and asked Eilish if she could handle another orange juice. She gave him a stiff smile. He went to the bar where he had a couple of whiskey shots while waiting for the pints to settle. The barmaid was smirking, and her face didn't seem so round. She asked if he was having fun, and he said, "It's a bloody blast."

A young couple entered the bar. Dick didn't recognize them. He felt he was losing touch with the place. Every time he returned there were more strangers.

At the table, he made sure he was sitting straight. He guzzled some of his pint, and it made a loud noise when he put it on the table. He stared at it until the Guinness stopped swaying in the glass. His brother asked if he was okay. Eilish said that maybe he should come back to the house and eat something. Dick looked at her and thought 'You're so bloody grey.'

He said, "My brother was supposed to come to London you know, we had it all planned. His bags were packed."

Enda was watching him from over his glass. He said, "Come on, Dick."

Dick said, "It needs to be said."

Eilish didn't look surprised or alarmed. Whenever Dick had imagined speaking his mind, he'd pictured her worried. She'd bite her lip and tell him she was sorry. And his brother would be in the background, subdued and happy. Maybe he'd shrug at Eilish if to say, *Dick knows.* But there was not a crease in this woman's face. Her grey eyes had narrowed as if Dick had grown smaller on the stool.

"It was the quickest pregnancy I ever heard of," Dick said.

"Enough, Dick," Enda said, and Eilish said, "Do you want to know the truth?"

Enda told her to stop, but she didn't listen.

She said, "It wasn't my idea to get pregnant."

Dick laughed, but his mirth didn't last long. His brother was stone faced. He'd sat back and he wasn't looking at Dick anymore. Edna seemed a hundred miles away and there was nothing between the brothers except Eilish's words. Dick must have paled when Eilish said, "He couldn't listen to your drunken dribble anymore. You're all talk. How could he risk everything for that?"

Dick wanted to disappear when his brother looked at him. Every holiday, he had seen the same disappointment on his brother's face, and he'd never considered it was directed at him. Still, Dick refused to believe it.

"It's a stupid reason to have a baby."

Enda's hand found Eilish's. "It's not all about you," he said

Dick felt as if he was floating somewhere dark and quiet. Enda was staring at the table when Eilish said, "We should go." He finished his pint and was putting on his jacket when he told Dick to come home when he was ready. Dick nodded, and knew he wouldn't stray from the hotel that night. He felt old and worn. He thought the future had been settled, and he'd be alone while Enda would have his family here. There'd be Christmas cards sent every now and again, but Dick wouldn't come back to visit, not with Eilish and her stern way.

He had no idea that he would move home in five years with two suitcases and a bad back. He'd take a room upstairs and spend most of his time in the bar. The morning of his brother's accident in the quarry, Dick's head would be on fire and his stomach raw. Still, after hearing the news he'd manage to walk to his brother's house, and stand for long minutes on the corner of the street before retreating in tears. Dick would tell no one about the feeling of being watched when he ambled back over the bridge desolate and full of regret. He'd pause with the river below him and stare at our Lady, afraid to get any closer but unwilling to step away from the line of her gaze.

In the years to come, whether or not Dick believed the statue had been looking at him depended on his mood, though he would not touch a drop of alcohol that day or the next. Nor would he linger long at his brother's funeral where the Sacred Heart still hung on the wall.

Six months sober, he'd receive a phone call from Eilish asking him to come. The widow's eyes would bear the redness of tears and her skin the pale pallor of sleepless nights when she'd open the door to him and say, "I can't do it alone."

The simple admission would make Dick breathless. For a moment, he would be unable to speak to the dark haired boy watching them from the kitchen door.

The Taste of Salt

AT TWENTY-THREE, LOU COULD have been taken for a fifteen year old if not for his eyes. He was prone to stare and had an air of malice that made people forget how slight he was. He had an idea that he made others uncomfortable but he didn't think too much of it. He was as reluctant to wonder why people behaved the way they do, as he was to think about himself. If he did, he would understand that Hagan had shaped him into the quiet insular man he was. For most things he did, there was an element of shame, though he would not have understood it as such. He believed he was shy and incapable of understanding his surroundings to the full extent. He supposed his inability to re-visualize the world (a phrase Richmond had used that he always remembered) had left him with an erring point of view. There were things he would never comprehend, not only other people's behavior but his own. Why for example did he find an adrenalin rush from taking what was not his? He stole small things at first, knives and glasses from the café he worked in, a little cash here and there, a phone left on the counter.

It was the invisibility of thievery that he loved, the fact that he could get away with doing something that no one else saw, and no one bar Joe would be privy too. As a child, Lou had learned to hate attention. Attention was Hagan shouting at him and pulling him from his seat. Attention was her hands pinching his cheeks and her harsh voice flowing over him. Once he'd tried to loosen her grasp on his cheeks by moving his head this way and that, like a dog trying to break free from its leash and his teeth ended up on the skin between her thumb and pointer finger. He tasted the salt of her, and knew what he had done when it was too late. He could never understand how he had bitten her; a blank moment and her flesh was between his teeth. It was not anger that made him do it. He'd never felt angry until he saw Joe laid out cold, and then Lou had the urge to tug at Joe's suit and shout at him to wake up.

If Lou had never met Hagan, if life had led him on a different path, he would have cried and Joe's mother might have stood beside him, instead of watching him from the couch. Between them was the coffin that held her son. She could not stay in the room long. Throughout the day, she would sit on the couch until she felt as if the very air was being squeezed from her. Her head would get light and she would start to imagine what it would be like to scream and tear at the dead boy in front of her. She wanted to pull him from the coffin, lay him over her, like she did when he was a baby. All those scraped knees, the tearful embraces, how could they have led to this? Her scramble from the room would be urgent and distressing.

Joe's father, balding, the buttons of his white shirt straining under his belly, was sitting in the kitchen getting steadily drunk. His hands were on the table and his gaze kept on his can of beer. He had not uttered a word all day and refused to go to the sitting room. He could not look at his son like that. He wasn't strong enough or drunk enough. Neighbors patted him on the shoulder and moved towards the open back door to chat or smoke, ignoring the ashtray full of cigarettes with the blue trails issuing from it.

At the living room door, mourners paused with the sight of Lou. He was known as a trouble maker and was too pale and drawn in the face for comfort. His knuckles shone white against the black lacquer of the coffin. There was an air of tension.

"It was like stepping around broken glass," an elderly neighbor would say, "Stan in the kitchen and Lou Denison in the living room. We were all afraid of what might happen…"

Lou didn't think of it. He thought of nothing, but his too-still friend.

There was a time when Lou didn't know Joe, but he couldn't remember. They'd been best friends since they were six. Lou felt as if his insides had been scooped out. He was a husk staring at Joe in his only suit that was too short in the legs now. On the couch in front of him sat Maggie, a tiny woman with white hair. Her black dress was baggy around the belly and waist. She held her handbag on her knees. She was a nonagenarian and lived in one of the smaller houses around the corner. She had been sitting for hours with her elderly neighbor, Nigel.

Nigel Morris wore a grey suit and had gnarled hands. Sister Margaret, an elegant nun from the secondary school, had stood beside Lou at one stage and said that he could take a break if he wanted. Maggie was not going anywhere. She insisted that she would stay for the night. She'd been seventy when Joe was born and had never thought she would out-live him. There were no relations to take a permanent place in the living room. Neighbors drifted in and out. The stools around the edge of the room were empty. In this house there had just been the parents, Stan and Nora, and their son Joe. Growing up, Lou and Joe had shared a feeling of isolation. But Joe had had graveyards to visit. His maternal grandparents were buried three miles up the road and his father's parents were in Co. Meath. There were names and stories to root him. While Lou's mother refused to talk about her family.

She did not come to the wake either. He would discover this when he returned home red–eyed and feeling the ripening of an anger that would never leave. She'd tell him she hadn't been able to bring herself to walk the few hundred yards to Joe's house. It scared her too much.

"What about me? Didn't you think I was fucking scared?" he'd say and her surprise would infuriate him.

He had always been quiet. He had wandered in and out of her house without demands. His earliest memory was standing at the kitchen, a room of dark colors and dust. His hand was reaching towards the glass door and the figure on the other side moving away. He knew it had to have been his mother. After school, he'd come home to find soggy tomato sandwiches on the table for him. He would pass them by and take the soiled pants from his bag and put them in the washing machine before his mother saw them. She must have seen them later, but she never said anything.

Ester Raines was beside Lou now. He hadn't noticed her arrival. She sighed. After a moment she said, "I'm so sorry Lou." She was in her late sixties, small and firmly built. Her hair was cut tight, curled and dyed red. Lou nodded. The urge to cry would come and go. Ester was watching him with soft eyes that made him feel young and vulnerable. If things had been different, he might have gone for the hug that her gaze offered. Ester was a kind woman. She'd worked in the primary school as a cleaner when Lou was there. She'd found him in the playground once and asked, "What's wrong, what's happening?"

He hadn't known how to answer. His second teacher Richmond had asked something similar. He'd tried to help Lou, but Lou hated the fuzzy letters, the smell and quietness of the classroom and the sight of Richmond's finger on the page.

Ester was gone. Joe's mother trembled as she left the room. An empty fire place stood behind Lou. Against the wall were the small stools that had been borrowed from the local pub. A small television stood in the left corner, mute and cheerless. Over the fireplace was a photo of Joe as a baby with his dark tuft of hair and wide grin. On the wall to the right of the mantle, there was an image of Joe in his communion suit standing outside the church. He looked pious with hands joined and a shy smile. In Lou's house, there was a picture of Lou and Joe standing together. Lou's piousness was not so convincing with his runny nose and sideways glance towards what might have been his mother. His father had stopped coming home months before. His absence was not discussed on that day or later when the photo had been framed and hung on the wall. To Lou's right and facing the living room door was a photo of Joe in his graduation suit. He was standing by the front door and smiling. His fringe was long and hanging over one eye. Lou had not been there that night. He'd dropped out of school at fourteen. Joe had asked him to come. "At least have one drink with me."

Lou said he'd rather die than hang out with those wankers. Besides he didn't drink, he was a smoker. At sixteen, the thumb and pointer finger on both hands were nicotine stained from rolling cigarettes and joints. They seemed an unlikely pair. Dark haired handsome Joe was the life of the party, the budding musician and impersonator of teachers. He'd liked attention and notice, while Lou was quiet. To some people, he seemed dull and maybe a little dimwitted. But the boys were inseparable. They moved to Dublin the first chance they got. By the time they'd left the village, the primary school had been extended. There were two more teachers to handle the growing population of children from the housing estates. Hagan no longer had the first four years to teach. In Lou and Joe's day, this comprised of only fifteen children. Of all of them, Lou was the one she liked to send to the corner for being stupid, an *eejit, not being able to read at seven. No, you cannot go to the bathroom.*

Joe had made Lou laugh at school. He had been funny and reckless. The manic moods and anxiety came later. In Dublin, Joe might be high on his chances of success. He'd spend the day talking about being discovered busking on Grafton Street. He would be another Glen Hansard, a singer, songwriter made big by the city. But the next week he might not get out of bed with the fear of it all.

The last time Lou talked to him was from a Dublin garda station. "I have to pay a fine," Lou said. "They won't press charges."

"This time," Joe said.

"Alright, can you come or not?"

What had Joe said then, nothing? Had he just hung up? Had he known what he was doing when he cycled through the red light on a busy street?

Lou shivered. The evening had gotten cold. There was a slight wind that blew into the hall whenever the door opened. Lou was aware of the flutter of clothes and the youthful murmurs the moment they arrived. Maggie gazed at them standing at the living room door. Their presence saddened her further. She was reminded of everything stolen from the boy lying in front of her. Sinead Geraghty had long blonde hair and rings on every finger. Her supple body was hidden under a black coat that looked big enough to be her father's. With her, was shy dark-haired Megan Flood in her flea coat and

Doc Martins, her brother Miles, bulky-bodied with a shaved head, Richard Foley with his mop of thick brown hair and an old suit, Joanne Walsh, a brunette with bad skin, and her boyfriend Gerald Daley with long hair and tight jeans. Sinead was the first to approach the coffin. Her movements were graceful compared to the shuffling of the others. Lou didn't look up. He felt as if he was under water, waiting for a break in air. They didn't really know him but it was easy to forget this, to accept their wariness as reasonable. There was a temptation to step back from the coffin, to surrender to them, but he couldn't move back from Joe. His hand felt glued to the hard wood. Maybe this was the only thing keeping him steady. Joanne thought his lack of acknowledgment was the reason for her discomfort, the way he had of ignoring you, or looking at you as if he saw right through you. She wanted to shove him and say, "Hey." The boys were pissed that he was taking so much room, that he thought himself so fucking important as to stand with his legs sprawled and his hands on the coffin. None of them thought anything of Megan going to the other side of Lou, and away from them. Her dark hair fell over her face and she was crying when her pale hand covered Lou's. She had no rings, and her touch was so light he was afraid to move and scare her away. Even his breathing seemed intrusive, while the air had tightened around the others. They must have been surprised, glancing at the joined hands every so often but they did nothing. When Megan slid her hand away, Lou closed his eyes and listened to her retreat and was afraid he might cry.

Alone, his gaze drifted to the window covered with a net curtain. Outside, he could see the outline of the houses across the street. Six steps and you'd get from one pavement to the other. He and Joe had counted it as boys. The houses across the street were identical two story houses with small square gardens and a sloping driveway. Lou noticed the net curtain was slightly yellow in places. The place smelled of stale cigarettes. He would have liked to smoke but he couldn't abandon Joe. And in any case, the thought of leaving the room and walking through the bodies was too much. Megan and the gang might be in the narrow hall or the kitchen. Lou didn't know what he might say to her and her brief kindness was enough to hold onto for now.

His legs were stiff from standing all day. He was suddenly conscious of his dry mouth and empty stomach. The mirror in the hall reflected the back of Nora Hession's lank brown hair when she paused to look at him. She wore a long shapeless black dress and a black cardigan. She walked into the room and stood beside Lou instead of taking her place on the couch. The smell of cigarettes was intoxicating. Her breathing seemed labored.

"Don't you want to sit down?" she said.

In a glance, he saw pale skin and tired blue eyes. She had a broadening face and lines on her forehead and at the sides of her mouth. He didn't know how to read her. The words reached him seconds after they were spoken. He'd been unable to grasp the intonation, concern or impatience? He would probably have guessed the latter, but he was too tired to think. It was dark outside and he stepped back and sat on the low stool. He was surprised when she took the seat beside him, but not altogether unhappy. It was nice to have her there, to smell the familiar scent and to share the silence. Usually, she made him nervous, but he was at ease now. She wasn't looking at him. They had Joe in common.

When she said, "You were always trouble," Lou imagined he heard Joe laugh. "She doesn't know the half of it," he would have said if he was alive. He would have nudged Lou too, loosened him up, made him smile, but Joe wasn't there and Lou was stiff and unable to move a single muscle.

"I know he was on his way to see you." When she looked at him he felt the chill in her gaze. He wished she would hit him. He imagined the sound of the slap, the reddening of his cheek. He imagined her striking him again and again and he wouldn't resist. Silently he begged for her to call Stan with his beer breathe and big hands. Stan could pull Lou from the stool and thump him hard enough to break something inside. The mourners would watch from the door. They'd be drawn from the kitchen or from the small square patch at front and back where they congregated to smoke. No one would say anything because no one ever did. But she didn't hit him or call Stan. She sighed and rose from the stool.

The Shape of Longing

"I HAVEN'T SEEN YOU in a while," I said to the bar-girl. She had wide cheeks and large vacant eyes. She made me think of crocodile peeking out of the water, or is that an alligator? Whatever it was, I never liked her. She was sullen and lazy, and was rinsing the glasses and putting them in the washer when I stumbled in. Ashtrays were piled up on the counter and the lights were glaring bright so I saw the sweat on her forehead.

"Yeah," she said. "I was away and now I'm back."

I didn't know if she was mocking or just making a statement. She was not inclined to smile much. There were some people at the back of the pub and a broad back on one of the stools that I didn't want to look at too closely.

"Last orders are done," she said. I told her that was okay. I just wanted a naggin for take-out. I realized I was clutching the money in my coat pocket so tight my fingers hurt. The bar-girl had just put a glass in the washer when I heard, "Ann Lavin or is it Mahoney by now? Surely he's divorced you."

There was a sprinkling of laughter, and I closed my eyes and murmured, "Shit." His voice had deepened in the years since I'd wiped his bum and fed him his meals but there was no mistaking it.

"What are you doing?" he said, when he'd reached the bar seat beside me, and draped his hands over the back. You couldn't say we looked alike. I had fair hair and was small-boned and delicate. He wasn't much taller than me but he was large, going onto fat, and he had our father's auburn hair. His eyes were a darker, moodier brown than mine. He smelt of cigarettes and beer, but he was steady enough to hold contempt. The bar-girl had put my bottle on the counter and was waiting for the money. I wanted to get away, but my hand had gone rigid and I thought even if could get it out in the open, I wouldn't be able to ease my fingers.

"When was the last time you saw Bernadette?" he said.

The bar-girl was still watching us, only she wasn't a girl anymore I realized. There were lines sprouting from her eyes and I wondered how long she'd been away. It was probably the same amount of time since I'd seen Bernadette. The thought made my fingers ease.

"Ann," Ryan said, and I stepped forward to leave the money on the counter and grab the bottle.

"She's just a child," he said.

He was looking at me, as if he had a clue of what I'd been through. I told him to get lost and mind his own business.

"It is my business," he said. "Ma's in bits."

"She didn't care as long as I stayed in that house pretending to be happy."

"Pretending to be sober you mean?"

"You don't have a clue what you're talking about."

He grabbed my arm when I started to leave.

"It's been sixteen months," he said and I pulled away. I didn't bother tell him that I knew exactly how long it was before going for the door. Outside, the rain was falling heavily but I didn't care. Tomorrow, my brother Ryan would go to my parents and tell them he'd seen me late at the pub.

"She was crawling out for drink," he'd probably say and Ma would doubtless cry from the shame of me abandoning her granddaughter. They all think it's a choice you make, as if out of the blue you decide to leave your family, when in reality these decisions are years in the making.

As a girl, I used to stand by my brother's bedroom door at night. He was four years younger than me, and since I could remember, he was my responsibility. My parents were busy with the pub. My brother slept on his back with his arms flung over his head. In the hall-light his skin looked golden and I would have liked to touch his soft cheeks and nose. But I was too nervous of waking him, because then I could not love him. He had demanding hands, and was constantly hungry. I'd finish washing the dishes from dinner, and he'd ask for a sandwich or some fruit, and tell Ma if I didn't do what he wanted. He knew Ma was too busy with the customers to have to worry about her younger son, and I would get into trouble if he ran to the bar.

"This is no place for kids," she'd say, though we hardly lived separate from it. The kitchen was behind the bar, and on the busy nights I wouldn't hear the television, or be able to sleep in my tiny box room above it. I was sure I'd heard footsteps some nights coming up the stairs towards me. I'd lie in bed stiff with fright, imagining the door opening to a stranger. Maybe, it would be one of those girls I'd seen in the lounge, who laughed without covering their mouths. I tried to imagine what they wanted to say to me, if they would tell me that it was easy to sit at a table being squashed on both sides. Maybe they would tell me that it was better up here in the quiet room. But I wouldn't have believed them.

After I left my daughter, I imagined her lying in bed waiting for the door to open just as I had done, but I didn't feel guilty because I'd remember that no matter how much I wanted someone to appear I'd drifted to sleep eventually.

To get to my daughter from my house, I have to walk past the housing estate, and the shop, and over the bridge to the Main Street. She is in a white house across the road from the Dun Maeve hotel, right smack in the middle of town. No matter where I'm going I can't avoid it. Maybe that's why Maurice never wanted to move. We could have bought a bigger place. Months after Bernadette was born, I used to ask about a garden, or a house with bigger windows. He said he was born on Main Street, and never wanted to leave, and now his house is like an eye watching everything. The living room windows look straight onto the street. If you wanted to, you could reach out and touch the people passing by, but when they glance in they see nothing but their reflection. I hid in that house for a long time or was kept hidden, I'm not sure which. Sometimes it's hard to remember exactly what happened. I do know I had no choice to leave. Maybe I should have had the decency to move away from town so my daughter wouldn't see me. She could believe her mother was searching for her. While she looked at photos, she'd wonder what accident befell me to keep us apart. Instead she can look up from her homework and see me walk past her living room window. Her heart must stop when she sees me but it re-starts.

When I first left, my husband said our daughter was like a little magpie, collecting things of mine that lay around the house and hiding them in her room. He said when she asked where I was, he couldn't answer. He'd change the subject and he would see her confusion and hurt. It was terrible for her to come back and see more of me disappear, my boots from the front door, the coat from the closet, my favorite mug. He said I should have taken everything at once and left town so she would not have to see me. He tried to make me guilty in my small house with the light streaming through the kitchen window and the view of the bay. But I was tired of feeling guilty and I told him I was not going anywhere.

He said, "But what can I tell Bernadette."

I said, "Tell her to be angry."

When I was sixteen, my mother and I were in the kitchen together. I watched her make toast and tea. I had my breakfast before me and had been sitting at the table when she came in. The silence was not new, but it was the first time I thought of it. I thought if my brother was there she would be talking. She'd ask me if he was fed, if his gear was ready for football, if he'd had a snack. I watched my mother and silently begged her to say something but she sat across from me and ate her toast as I if I wasn't there. I wanted to throw my juice in her face and things might have been different if I did. If I'd made my mother look at me, I might have wanted more.

The pub my parents owned had seats and tables of dark wood, plastic flowers on the window sill and a fire across from the main door. The door opened up to a wide gravel car park. There were fields on every side, and Coolaney Mountain behind with roads as thin as thread. I probably looked like child behind the bar with my thin frame and fair hair but I was eighteen when I started work there.

On Sunday afternoons, I had the place to myself while my family went to 11 o'clock mass. I used to pretend to go to the earlier service. I dressed while my family slept, and cycled to the old graveyard to meet Maurice Lavin. When I was supposed to be kneeling at the pews with my hands joined, he was kissing me. The stone wall shook with our weight, while hymns were being sung.

Maurice had red hair and broad shoulders. We started seeing each other when he asked me to dance at the youth club disco. His hands were light on my back, and after a few steps my nerves left me. By the end of the song, my head was on his shoulder and my eyes were closed. He was the only person I talked to about my mother. I told him I would sometimes catch her staring at me with a clouded look on her face as if she had no idea who I was.

"You were her first," he said once. We were older then. We'd taken a drive in his car and had stopped by the beach. I was sitting against him with his arm around my waist. At first I didn't know what he meant and then I did, and I imagined my mother pulling at her skin trying to get me out. The pain was a low heavy ball in my stomach. He was so sorry when I cried, and held me for a long time. I thought we would always be together, but we were only children grasping at each other.

In the months before I left Maurice, we hardly said a word to each other. He slept in the spare room and I heard his movements in the morning as he dressed and got our daughter up. I'd listen to their voices, and the clinking of plates and glasses. Eventually I would feel my daughter at my bedroom door and I'd get scared that she might call to me.

"Mammy," she would have said and I would have pretended not to hear. I hated myself for the cowardice but this only made me curl tighter in the bed.

From the moment my daughter was born, she made me feel like running away. The way she looked at me was so open I thought she might swallow me whole.

I thought of my mother too. You'd think that would make me reach out, but it didn't, and eventually my daughter would step back, and I would hear the front door close behind her. Maurice would walk her through the village and across the bridge, past his business, 'Lavin's Construction,' and through the housing estate to get to her school. At the back gate of the school, there was a view of the bay and it was possible to see the dust from his quarry.

On my last morning with them, our phone started ringing seconds before they left the house. Maurice ignored it. He was probably in a rush and thought it was his office asking where he was. When it stopped and started again, I took the phone off the hook and replaced it without a word. Then I lay the receiver on the table, and crawled back to bed. I know now that it was his secretary calling from his office, and she was sobbing.

When I think of that morning, it's hard to know where to put the son and wife. Raymond was around five then, so maybe he was in the playground when the ambulance passed or he was on his way to school holding Eilish's hand. They would have stopped to watch the ambulance disappear around the bend. Eilish might have felt a strange sickness, but she would have brushed it aside to bring her boy to school. She wouldn't have waited around with the other mothers, whispering about what might have happened. My husband's friend was above gossip and whispering. I thought her old at thirty-three with hard grey eyes and a thickening body. She would have kissed her son and walked home. Maurice and Eilish would not have seen each other, until he knocked on the door with the police to tell her the news. I imagine she would have fallen in a heap onto the floor and screeched. Maurice would have waited until she'd quietened before going to her.

He was dried out and empty by the time he stood at my bedroom door. I woke to his presence. His breathing filled the room, and there was a weight to it that I had never felt before. It made me nervous. He said my name and I heard the disgust. He said, "Look at me."

I pulled the covers from my face and sat up. He looked so angry. His jaws were tight and his face was a scarlet red. I noticed his eyes were sore-looking from crying and his fists were clenched. He said, "Enda Hurley was killed today."

For a minute I thought, 'This isn't real, I'm dreaming in the hotel bed,' but there was no warm body beside me. I felt the goosebumps on my skin and the pain in my head and I knew I was awake, though I still couldn't believe it. I'd only seen Enda the previous night and I couldn't reconcile the memory of his face with death. Maurice was talking through my confusion. He said that Enda fell asleep on the digger. That was the only way to explain how he'd gone over the edge. Stan Hession shouted at him, but Enda's head was down and he didn't react.

"You've made a fool of us, and now Raymond has no father." He paused before saying, "God help Eilish." I hated the sound of her name coming from his lips. It was her fault Enda was out, her and my husband's. I said as much. I was sitting up in my T-shirt and underwear. I looked a mess. I could feel it in the way he glared at me. I told him, "None of this would have happened if you didn't phone Eilish. Why didn't you look for me, why couldn't you do something for once instead of having someone else do it for you?"

I scrambled from the bed and picked my jeans off the floor. My clothes stank of cigarettes, but I didn't care. I wanted to shove the truth in his face. He was watching me as if I had sprouted a second head. He said, "How could I look for you and leave Bernadette alone?"

"You always use her as an excuse."

"She's your fucking daughter."

I couldn't remember the last time Maurice cursed. He lacked the vehemence for it. "Jesus," he said and ran his hand through thinning red hair. He looked as if he might cry and it hit me that Enda was dead. They must have gotten Raymond from school. I couldn't ask. My head was throbbing and my stomach felt sick. The thought of Enda made me sit on the end of the bed.

"I want you out of this house," Maurice said. He didn't answer when I asked why he had to wait until Enda was killed. Why didn't he tell me weeks ago?

I started hearing Eilish's name soon after Bernadette was born. She was an environmental engineer and had come from Castlebar to do work in the quarry. Eilish had lost her parents young, and I'm sure this was the first thing Maurice loved about her. When he first brought Eilish to our house I was scared of her. She had coolness about her from being able to survive her tragedy. Maybe when you got to know her there was more than just the disaster. There might have been some softness but I didn't know her well enough, and I never saw a hint of it.

Enda Hurley was in our year at school. He was always beautiful with blonde hair and bright blue eyes. When we were in our final year, Enda's mother was found walking through the village in her nightdress. Some people said Mrs. Hurley was sick from grief from losing her husband. Others said, she'd always been a little strange. Everyone said, it wasn't fair that his older brother Dick took off for London and left Enda alone to take care of her. They'd been a common sight running around together as boys, and for years after his brother's departure, Enda was hardly seen.

I had forgotten him until one Friday night Maurice mentioned giving him a job in the quarry. Bernadette was around four then. Maurice refused to go out and leave her with a babysitter or deal with having to keep her quiet in the restaurant, so Eilish came to us. She was sitting across from him when he mentioned Enda and she'd shrugged and was about to say something when I piped in, "You should meet him."

She paused to look at me and for a moment I thought she would go back to her conversation without acknowledgment but she said, "Who?"

"Enda of course," I looked at Maurice and said, "Why didn't we think of it before."

"Because we're not kids," he said, and I wanted to tell him that was exactly how he was acting. Instead I told Eilish that she couldn't get better than Enda Hurley and I had a photo to prove it. I rose and ignored Eilish's protests, but Maurice's glare made me feel weak-kneed. He was holding Bernadette in his arms. She always fell asleep on him and he would bring her to bed. If Eilish was around I would follow him to the bedroom, because I didn't like being alone with her. She reminded me of my mother. I heard him mumble something when I left the room, but they were quiet when I returned. Eilish was sitting back from the table with her head lowered. She looked uncomfortable, and I was sure I'd interrupted something. The embarrassment made it hard to find Enda, despite his broad shoulders and direct stare. I pointed him out to her. I repeated that he was a great guy and said, "He's not bad looking either."

Eilish's nod was reluctant, but it was a nod all the same. You would think I would feel some victory but I didn't. I just felt tired. I said, "He's been taking care of his mother for years."

"A Mammy's boy," Eilish said with more than a little disdain. She'd started playing around with her food. Pasta dishes lay on the table along with a half-eaten salad. Bernadette had sauce all over her face. I knew she wouldn't be washed until tomorrow, and she'd scream then.

"Have you been listening at all?" I said.

The fork stilled in her hands and her eyebrows lifted with my tone.

"He is taking care of her, not the other way around. He's a martyr."

Maurice laughed and told me not to be ridiculous.

"Who's being ridiculous?" I said. "You think I'm an idiot and I don't know what's going on?"

Maurice shifted in his seat and was about to say something but before he had a chance Eilish said, "Okay."

"Okay what?" Maurice said.

"Okay, I'll meet him."

"Don't be stupid," he said and Eilish's gaze was on my daughter when she said it's not stupid.

I've often imagined Eilish and Enda's first meeting. Like her, he had a subdued confidence so I think they would have sized each other up quietly. Then he would have smiled and said hello and she would have been tongue tied for the first time in her life.

Not long after she agreed to meet Enda, Eilish stopped coming for dinners. "She's busy," Maurice told me when I enquired as to why she never graced us with her presence anymore.

"So the match-making worked," I said, when we received the invitation.

Maurice said apparently. He was getting Bernadette ready to take to his parents' house. They went most Saturdays. I was invited but I didn't leave the house much then. I rarely saw Maurice during the week. Most nights I would be in bed before he came home from work. We might have carried on like that forever, with the two of us hardly saying a word and sharing the responsibility of Bernadette if not for the wedding.

The emptiness of the church made the priest's voice echo. Enda's brother Dick was sitting on the other side of the church from us. His dark hair was slicked back and his suit slightly creased. Maurice stood between him and me. Maurice frowned during most of the ceremony. His gaze was held on Eilish in the cream dress that came to her ankles and rose slightly in the middle. It seemed improbable that the square shouldered unsmiling girl we'd had dinner with was the same woman who held her hand out for her wedding ring. She was smiling and radiant. Enda was handsome. He'd grown larger through the years, not fat, just solid and more present. They looked like a fine couple by the altar with their hands joined.

The restaurant in the hotel had wide windows that looked out into the main avenue. A patch of green was to the right. The road was hidden by a stone wall so the tops of cars were the only evidence of life going on else-where. At the table, we toasted the bride and groom. Eilish had a flute of water. Enda sipped his champagne with his hand on her back. His blonde hair was to his shoulders and his tie loose. He didn't seem a man inclined to talk much, but he looked content as he surveyed the menu and leaned towards his new wife to ask what she wanted.

After we ordered, Dick raised his glass and said, "To Maurice, the match maker."

Maurice glanced at me, but said nothing, and neither did Eilish. Dick's voice had made her straighten in her seat and her glance towards him was cursory, so I had the impression she didn't care enough to set him straight. We touched glasses and all the while Enda was watching his brother. It was impossible to know what he was thinking. The smile was there, but the eyes were clouded and wary. Dick was a different kind of man to his brother. Enda was solid where Dick was all sinewy arms and legs. Dick's dark hair fell over his forehead. He had a long thin face.

"You must be grateful, Enda. You wouldn't have a job or a wife without him."

Enda said, "Okay, Dick."

"Well isn't it true, the job in the quarry is a blessing these days."

Enda's smile was stiff and didn't disguise the anger. His wife squeezed his hand. There was a second of silence when Dick mumbled, "A top notch guy," and everyone chose to ignore him.

Eilish said, "We're off to Greece tomorrow, if I can handle the ride."

Enda said he hoped so since it would be his first time out of the country.

"You might not come back," Maurice said.

Dick said it was hard alright, to come back once you've left. He always felt like a fish out of water. He took a long drink of his wine, and said that if Maggie wasn't enough to keep him away from London, nothing would be. It was in general agreement that it was crazy that it was her third term. When the dinner arrived, Eilish was saying that people forgot everything after the Falklands.

"People have short memories," Maurice said, and I thought that wasn't true at all.

During lulls in conversation, Dick ordered more wine. He was going back to the grind tomorrow, he said and it was time to celebrate. I wasn't surprised when Eilish stood and said she'd had enough and had to lie down. Enda said he'd join her.

"Ah come on," Dick said.

Enda was already following his wife and he didn't look back.

"Well, we haven't finished yet, have we?" Dick said.

Maurice looked at him long and hard, before saying "Yes, we have."

He rose and with a hand on my arm pulled me up. I was led to our room by my husband. Inside he told me to rest while he made some calls. It was a Friday, and work would keep him busy for a while. I'd had wine with dinner and my head was spinning. It was a warm May Day, and I decided to go for a walk. I wonder now if I was looking for him because I'd gone to the restaurant and then the bar, and I remember how restless I was before I stepped into the garden and saw him sitting on the bench smoking. He smiled when he saw me. There was laughter from inside the foyer, and my husband was in one of the rooms upstairs, but I didn't care.

"That was great craic," Dick said, when I sat beside him. I said I didn't expect anything less. It was nice to see him laugh. His eyes squinted and he looked younger. He threw his cigarette on the ground and stamped on it. Against the bench I was given a view of his slumping back and saw the sweat marks on his shirt.

"Eight fucking years I waited for him in London and when the mother dies, she's pregnant." His words robbed me of the notion of him as a boy. With all his withering, he had a boyish, innocent way about him. He brushed my arm, when he sat back. His navy eyes were watery and his face glistened with drink. He looked pitiful and sad. After a while he said, "Is this what you expected?"

"With the wedding?" I said and he smiled and said, "No, life, did you think you'd live on Main Street. Did you think that would be it?"

"I don't know."

He looked at me for a while and I had to suppress an urge to laugh. "Ah come on, as a kid, did you not dream of something?" he said.

I tried to remember. The quiet when my brother was asleep was the only thing I longed for, but still I didn't seek it out. I didn't go anywhere else or dream of a different house that was not attached to a pub. It scared me to think of how little I'd wanted. He must have seen that because he smiled sadly and said that it was probably better not to have expectations.

"That's not true," I said. There was fear in his eyes when

he asked why, or maybe that came after I'd said, "Because then you feel nothing," and his hand slid over mine.

When my husband found me and Dick at the bar, he grabbed me by the arm. Dick stood and told him to leave me alone but my husband pushed him backward, spilling beer over his pants. Dick was leaning against the cushioned lounge with his arms spread and looked like a man tied to a cross when I glanced back from the bar door.

"I thought you were asleep," Maurice said through clenched teeth as he pulled me to the elevator. His grip on my arm tightened when I tried to get away.

I wasn't tired," I said, "and why should I have to stay in the room just because you were too busy?"

Then I told him that he couldn't fix anything. He only made it all worse.

Maurice said, "If you're so unhappy, you should leave."

But I didn't leave. Dick went back to London, and we went to the house on Main Street. Eilish's son was born the following October and my husband started to stay at work late. I'd collect Bernadette from school and we'd walk past Enda and Eilish's house. Sometimes, I'd see her walk with her son, and Bernadette would run to them. The delight would be clear on her face and I knew she'd seen him at other times, maybe Saturdays when she went to Maurice's parents, or those other afternoons he collected her from school and came home late.

On the street, Eilish would ask how I was and every now and then I had the urge to ask why she hadn't wanted Maurice, but I couldn't with Bernadette present.

My mother phoned one afternoon. She asked how I was and I told her, "I can't love my daughter because of you."

I don't remember when exactly this happened. It might have been when I started to walk at night. Bernadette and Maurice would be asleep, and I'd take off through the village and the estates and onwards to the church and left to the Saltpans, and there I would sit on the stone wall, turn off the flashlight, and listen to the lapping of the water. I'd stay out until it was bright and wandering home through the sleeping village I liked to pretend I was a tourist passing through. But I don't think I would have had the courage to answer my mother so honestly until Dick got off the bus from London, and I tapped the window and he stopped to look inside.

Enda came to the Dun Maeve hotel late. Dick had a room there with a double bed and clothes tossed on the floor. At night, when I left my house I went straight to the back door where he would let me in. I thought no one saw me but my husband must have been awake the night Enda found us. I imagine him standing in the dark and staring out the living room window as I walked across the road.

It was late when we heard the knocking and we started to giggle. "Dick, open the fucking door."

Dick's eyes widened when he heard his brother's voice and he said, "Uh oh."

Enda called him again, and none of my protests were enough to stop Dick from opening his door to his brother. I was beside him. "You need to go home," Enda said to me.

"Who says?" I knew I sounded childish but didn't care. My skin was red from Dick's fingers and my eyes glistened. "Your husband, remember him?"

"Why doesn't he come get me himself?"

"He's with your daughter."

"No," I said, "he isn't here because he doesn't care. He never has. He only cares what people think." Then it hit me and I couldn't help laugh. "He didn't want you to look for me. It was Eilish, wasn't it?"

Enda said it didn't matter. He looked bored. "I'm tired and I need to talk to my brother." After a second, he said, "Please, Ann."

Dick touched my hand and nodded when I glanced at him. He looked different in his brother's presence, more apologetic and soft, and I couldn't argue.

For a while, I thought my leaving Bernadette started then, but that was foolish. It started those nights above the pub when I'd hear the laughter and talk and feel loneliness that made me sink into the bed. I didn't know what I yearned for then, and in what shape the longing would come. When my daughter was born, I had the dark rooms and her hands, and the view of the whole world going on without me. And I reached for the closest thing at hand. Eilish would come on a Friday, and I'd ask her if she ever fucking laughed, and she would look at me with those stern eyes and say nothing. My husband would not take us to a restaurant. He liked to hold my daughter close to him and pretend I wasn't there. But I'd follow him when he brought Bernadette to bed and I'd ask him if he was going to tuck me in too. He would leave me sprawled and wine-stained over the covers. Sometimes I'd hear him apologize for his wife and her behavior, and I believe he brought Eilish to us, so she might pity him. But it didn't make her want him.

After the dinner at the wedding, I'd collapsed onto the bed. I'd heard my husband on the phone. He was talking to Eilish, who'd stood from the dinner table in her cream dress, and left. My husband sounded as if he might have been crying, but maybe not, maybe it was anger that I'd heard as I slipped out of the room.

At home that night everything was quiet, and I stood staring out the living window until it started to get bright but I didn't see Enda emerge. I don't know what time he went home, or what he said to his brother. The next morning my husband came home with the news of his death and I ran over to Dick's hotel room the first chance I got. I heard him sobbing behind the door and in that gloomy hall, I thought of Eilish walking her son home from school in the still quiet of late morning, and Bernadette staring out her classroom window, and my hands touched the door but I couldn't knock.

THE WRONG MAN

OF THE TWO FRIENDS, Moire was the wistful one. She was thin with pale skin. There were often rings under her dark eyes and a slouch to her shoulders, that made her look weak and disinterested. She didn't talk much to anyone, other than Ester, and liked to read. Ester wasn't interested in books. She sat her final exams for school without bothering to do much work. The results wouldn't have made any difference to her in any case. Her family couldn't afford to send her to college. Plans had been made for her to go to London. It was her mother's idea and Ester hadn't been willing to take away her excitement in writing letters to daughters of friends to secure a room. Nor did Ester want to imagine her life at home where she'd probably work in a shop and have to help her mother with her three younger brothers. Like her mother, Ester was wide shouldered but she had her father's sandy colored hair. She liked to cut it herself so her bangs were often crooked.

Both girls lived on the Donegal road outside Sligo town. Moire's family, the Hardings, had been land owners. Their estate had decreased in size with every generation, until Moire's father was left with the large house and a couple of acres he used for horses. Most of his time was spent in his law office in town. Ester's small bungalow was a half mile away. The girls had known each other since they were three years of age, when Ester's mother started cleaning the Harding's house twice a week. After her third child, she stopped working, but Ester would often be seen walking the road that on clear days held the shadow of Benbulben Mountain.

"Mammy got me a room with Janice Geraghty and a girl from Galway," Ester told Moire in their eighteenth year. The flat was in Finsbury Park. Ester said she didn't liked the sound of the place. Finsbury sounded rough and foreign.

Moire told her, "It'll be okay. I'm going with you."

They were sitting on the bed in Moire's room, cross-legged and facing each other. Moire's hair fell like a black curtain over her face. Dust mites rose in front of the uncovered window. No matter how bright the day, inside the house was dark with shadows settling into corners. The rooms were permeated with an ancient kind of quiet that Ester associated with grief.

"Will you be allowed?" Ester asked. She was afraid to hope. The thought of London alone had scared her. Moire said she had finished school and was going no matter what her father said. Mr. Harding was a broad man with dull brown eyes. Whenever he was home, he moved around the house in a dazed slow motion. Ester thought he'd hardly notice his daughter was gone, never mind try to stop her. He had tended towards moroseness since his first wife drowned. To see into her coffin, Ester had to get up on her tiptoes. But she'd done it, so there would be no secrets between her and her best friend. If Ester didn't look, she'd always wonder what knowledge was inside Moire's head and feel the breach from not knowing. Ester didn't figure the gap would be there regardless. A space existed in Moire where a mother had once been.

Two years after her mother drowned, Moire's father re-married. His new wife didn't seem to like the house. She stayed mostly in the kitchen where the large window looked out on the laneway and the Donegal road. She was a thin woman with short greying hair and a prominent chin. She was more ready to smile than Mr. Harding's first wife, but as reticent with words. Whenever Ester saw her, she was at the sink or sitting in the armchair by the kitchen stove. She'd been married before. A husband was lost some way or other and she was left with a boy, who took to the Harding horses straight away and within a few years was the sole charge.

Eight years older than the girls, Bernard was blond and tall, with beautiful blue eyes. Not long ago, Ester had been in the habit of writing his name diagonal to hers and drawing an arrow between them. Moire caught her once and the hurt in her voice surprised Ester.

She said, "You can't like him."

"You don't own him," Ester said.

Ester had felt the possessiveness in Moire's silent retreat and in the mood that hung over her for the rest of that day.

The day they spoke about England, after Ester had screamed with delight and hugged her friend, she'd gazed teasingly at Moire and said, "What about Bernard?"

And Moire looked at her for a long time before asking her to stop.

They took the boat to London. Moire would have afforded to fly, but not Ester with her younger brothers and her father working in the docks. Janice Geraghty's mother said that Moire could sleep on the couch in the sitting room and they'd still split the rent four ways. But Moire spent most nights giggling with Ester in her room. They were too excited to be troubled with the cramped space, filled with the wardrobe, a chest of drawers, and a bed just wide enough for the girls to sleep side by side.

Ester started work in the stationary shop within a few days. An accountancy firm in Islington employed Moire. Thanks to Bernard, she'd gotten an A in accountancy for her leaving certificate. He'd made up for Mr. Harding's lack of interest in education by taking her under his wing and helping her with her school work. Later, when she had surpassed him, he got her father to pay for private tuition. She had gotten A's in every subject except home economics.

The girls loved London but grew to hate the underground with its screeching noises and dizzying array of lines. It was easier to walk everywhere. They saw the sights and grew stiff outside Buckingham Palace, while mimicking the statue-like guards. At Trafalgar Square, they watched pigeons eating from a man's hand, and imagined the lives of the people they saw. Ester was never great at the stories. "They're on their honeymoon," she might say of a young couple. While, Moire would watch them for a minute before telling Ester that no, they were having an affair, they'd come to London for a weekend, leaving a partner in Dublin and in Germany, but they'd been careless. He'd phoned for the hotel at home, and the wife had seen the number on the bill. While she had confided in a close friend about her trip. Unfortunately, the friend was in love with the cuckold husband and told him everything. But he didn't fall into her arms. He jumped on a plane. Right now as they were walking hand in hand, their spouses were entering their hotel. Maybe they'd meet and fall in love, but maybe they'd sit in separate corners of the room.

"Cuckold, spouses," Ester said, surprised with the words, which seemed too adult or part of a reality they were not supposed to have reached yet.

In the evenings, they listened to the radio and danced around the dark shabby couch and mismatched armchairs. There were boys sometimes, neighbors or friends of their flatmates. Ester tended to fumble around the boys' questions. While Moire preferred to twirl around the room than be caught up in conversation. It was on one of those nights, when Moire had rebuffed a boy and escaped to their bedroom, that Ester first heard Ron's name.

"He's kind and interested," Moire said of her boss.

"And," Ester said.

Moire laughed, and said, "And nothing."

Later, Ester realized the word "interested" should have made her sit up and question Moire until the truth came out.

As the days shortened, Moire started working late and wouldn't get home until after 10. There were times when she stayed with co-workers because she missed the last bus. Ester heard names like Sharon or Emily and imagined English girls with singing voices and curled hair. She never conceived of an affair.

Before three months she came home to Moire packing her bags. Ester was sure Moire was going home because letters had come from Bernard. The envelopes with his name and address on the back had made Moire go into their shared room and quietly close the door. Ester had imagined they were filled with entreaties for her return. Bernard hadn't wanted her to go. Moire told Ester this and she had noticed a new quietness in him. But she couldn't say she pitied Bernard. He was someone who had rarely spoken to Ester. An unknown, he would have been revered more easily. There was never any sign of those letters afterwards. Ester had glanced through Moire's drawers and found nothing. Once she noticed some scraps of paper in the bin, torn so small, they looked as if they had been nibbled by a mouse.

"Why didn't you tell me you're going home?" Ester said.

Moire said, "I'm not. I'm moving in with Ron."

The shock winded Ester. The wardrobe doors were open and revealed unused hangers. Drawers had been pulled out, and looked desolate. The clothes in Moire's suitcase were neatly folded. She had taken her time. Ester wondered if Ron had let Moire leave work early, if she had hoped to be gone before Ester came back but then in the midst of packing Moire had started not to care.

Finally, Ester managed to say, "You can't."

"I can and I am," Moire told her.

"Please don't go. You're making a mistake," Ester said.

Moire zipped her suitcase. She said it was her life and she didn't expect Ester to understand.

The indifference in her voice was worse than anything. It left no room for argument. Ester felt as if she was disappearing in the room when Moire lifted the bank notes from the bed.

"This is my part of the rent," she said. "I don't want anyone to know I moved."

Ester said she wasn't surprised. What Moire was doing was beyond stupid. How could she move in with a man she hardly knew? She thought London was good for Moire, but obviously it had made her crazy.

Moire said she was not crazy, at least not anymore. Ester had no idea what Moire meant by that. Ester was on the verge of crying, while Moire remained calm and certain. For a while there was silence.

"At least tell me where you are going," Ester said.

Moire said, "I'll come see you Sunday."

On Sunday, Ester met Moire at the door of her flat. In a long grey dress and with her hair tied back, Moire looked a lot older than Ester felt. Ester's eyes were red from lack of sleep. For the first few nights alone, she'd cried in her bed.

She said, "I'm not going to have lunch and pretend everything's okay. I want to meet him and I want to see where you live, otherwise the next letter that comes from your home will be sent back unopened."

"No," Moire said, "I can't have you there yet. I need to settle. In a little while you can come for dinner, but not now."

She said, "Please Ester, you have to understand."

Ester went to close the door, and a pale hand came out to block it. "Okay, okay," Moire said.

The following week, Ester took the bus to Woodgreen. Moire's directions told her to take the first left. Gladstone Street was quiet. She was led past red bricked house with trees planted in gardens. There was a park somewhere around there. Moire said if Ester passed it, she'd gone too far. A woman in a grey coat pushed a pram past without looking at her. On a distant street, a car started and a horn sounded. Ester tried to remember what Moire told her about Ron. She'd said he was a qualified accountant. He'd studied somewhere South of London and moved up here ten years ago. "Ten," Ester had repeated. "What age is he?"

"What does that matter?" Moire said, and Ester told her that if it didn't matter so much she should be able to tell her.

"You have to give him a chance," Moire said, "I love him."

But Ester couldn't believe that. She saw it as a kind of need. Moire would fix on something and hold onto it, like a dog with a bone, not out of love or affection, but because of the uncertainty in her, the doubt that must have existed from losing a mother and the knowledge that one minute a person is there and then they are gone. For a while, she'd followed Bernard around too and refused to leave the house for days on end. Ester had caught her staring out the window waiting for him to come in from the horses with a kind of drawn want on her face. Ester wasn't sure when that ended, or if it did, but she was positive Bernard didn't take advantage of her dreaminess, not like Ron.

The house was a narrow red brick with a black rail fence and small gate. The tiny square garden had a tree starting to grow, and some yellow and red flowers around the edges. Moire opened the door in a long green skirt and grey sweater. She was bare foot and smiling. She looked happy to see Ester, as if her desertion hadn't happened, and Ester hadn't had to blackmail her into telling her where she lived.

She pulled Ester in through the hall. The walls were covered with patterned paper, the flowers looked like velvet. On a different day, Ester might have wanted to touch the soft wine-colored material, but today there was more irritation than wonder. She imagined her friend being brought here when she first met Ron and it made Ester uncomfortable.

Music was playing in the sitting room. The carpet was thick beige. Moire took Ester's jacket and asked if she found the house alright. Ester said yes fine, but kept the fright of the train station to herself. She pictured Moire laughing if she heard it and saying something like, "Silly you, you worry about everything."

The fire was on in the living room. Ron was standing in front of the armchair that had been pulled to the fireplace. The

room's main color was brown, dark for the couch and two armchairs, paler for the walls. There was a smell of cigarette smoke
and stuffiness to the air. Ron was an inch or two taller than
Moire. His slumped shoulders gave him a shy look, though his
face was open and smiling. He held Ester's gaze with a certainty
that annoyed her. His hair was black, side parted and longer
than was usual, though it was growing thin. His eyes were a
lighter brown than Moire's, and seemed kind, but Ester didn't
trust the narrow line of his lips.

His hand was moist. "Moire told me a lot about you,"
he said.

"Sit down," Moire said.

"Yes, yes," Ron said, gesturing to the couch behind her.
Ester obliged. He seemed relieved to take his seat on the armchair. Moire sat on the floor by his feet. For a while there was
silence. Ester had expected tea at least.

"Isn't the music lovely?" Moire finally said. "It's Miles
Davis, have you heard of him?" Before Ester could answer,
Moire started talking about a breakthrough in fusion he'd
made. Ester didn't know what fusion was, though apparently
it had something to do with Latin, which Ron corrected Moire
on.

"Latin American Countries, not Latin Countries," he'd
said at some point, and Moire glanced at him and said, "Of
course, that's what I meant."

All the time she spoke, Ron was smiling at Ester, as if to say
look what I've done and Moire's regurgitation of facts was anything other than that. To Ester, the music sounded disorganized.

There was no singer. She waited patiently for that. When Moire closed her eyes, Ester had a ferocious urge to pull Moire up from the floor and run out the door with her. She couldn't imagine Moire arguing. Instead she'd hit the fresh air and wake up to ask, "What happened. Who was I back there?"

But Ester couldn't move. The music stopped. Moire asked if anyone wanted tea. Ron jumped up and said he'd get it. Ester had the impression that he didn't want to be alone with her.

The kitchen was at the back of the living room, the doorway revealed a linoleum floor and two legs of a kitchen table. Once Ron had gone, the quietness was interrupted by a slamming press door and Ester asking, "What are you doing?"

She had slipped off the couch and was on the floor by her friend. "He's old enough to be your father."

"If he had me at fourteen," Moire said.

"I'm worried for you," Ester said, "You're not yourself."

"That's because I'm happy," Moire told her.

"So you weren't happy before this?" Ester said.

Moire leaned back on the chair. She seemed tired now. Without Ron beside her, she had become withdrawn. It frightened Ester and she reached for Moire's hand and asked her to come with her. Ester said everything will be alright; no one needs to know anything. People make mistakes all the time. She chatted about them going back to Ireland, or maybe trying someplace different in England. She'd heard Birmingham was fun. Anywhere was better than Woodgreen. She talked without thinking of the quiet that issued from the kitchen or the disbelief on Moire's face.

"I think you should go," Ron's voice shocked her. She turned to him holding a tray with a teapot, cups and a sugar bowl. When she'd think back on this scene, she'd view Moire's stricken face as the result of helplessness. Ester never wondered what she didn't know. Ron had a hold on Moire; Ester had no doubt about that. Yet that day in the house and in the weeks that followed, she never considered why Moire had started to cling to him, or that sharing a secret was the glue that kept them together.

He said, "Moire is happy here, you need to accept that."

Ester's face had reddened. She hadn't wanted him to know how she felt. Moire had pulled her hand away in the middle of her tirade, though Ester had thought nothing of it until now. She rose and mumbled an apology. Moire stood too.

"Maybe it's best if you go," Moire said. Ester followed her to the door and was surprised she was not crying. With her coat on, she asked if she could see Moire again.

Moire told her, "Ron's a good man. He won't stop you from coming. But you mustn't talk like that ever again, once we will forgive, but not twice."

When Ester had reached the gate, Moire called her and said, "If any letters come can you bring them to me?"

Ester said yes. She didn't want to think this was the reason Ron allowed her to visit, but she couldn't help it.

There weren't many letters. One came every two or three weeks, but the effect of their arrival was terrible on Ester. With the envelope in her hand, she felt as if Moire had died. The person the letter was intended for no longer existed.

Ester never saw Moire anywhere but Lymington Avenue. Ron was always there, maybe not in the living room, but in the kitchen cooking and making a racket, or upstairs where it seemed he would walk across the floor every now and again to remind Ester of his presence. There was an air of nervousness to Moire that Ester had always assumed was caused by Ron.

Whenever she brought a letter, Moire would take it and put it on the mantel. Once, Moire's father wrote. On the back of the envelope he'd written Malcolm Harding. Ester had stared at the name, trying to reconcile it with the image of the large silent man. She had always known him as Mister. "Hey, Mister Harding," she'd say as she came and went from the house. She couldn't imagine what he would have said. To her, the letter was cause for excitement, a key to Moire's father. It was possible too that whatever it held was a cure to the problem, that after so long living in his own world, he'd come back to help his daughter. Whatever was written on those pages would wake Moire up.

Ron answered the door that day. He said hello in a genial way and stepped back to let her in. The television was on. Moire was sitting on the couch with her legs curled up.

"Look," Ester said, brandishing the envelope, "Your Dad wrote."

Moire took the letter and put it on the mantel.

"Aren't you going to open it?" Ester said. Ron was standing at the living room door. His forehead was creased with worry.

"Maybe later," Moire said.

Ester managed not to cry until she was walking to the bus stop.

The next letter came weeks later. Ester thought of making the journey to Moire, only to see the letter put on the mantel. She had started to think all the messages from home were thrown into the fire when she left the house. Ron would have come in from the kitchen or down the stairs the moment the front door closed behind her. He would have lifted them up from the place he must have instructed Moire to put them. Without looking at her or giving her a moment to change her mind, he would have thrown the letters into the flames.

Ester opened the envelope. There was no steaming or carefulness, no need to cover her tracks. She would not continue her futile journey and be part of their ritual.

Moire,

You must have received Malcolm's letter and all the others too. I've stopped waiting to hear from you but how could you not write to your father. He's not well, and now he's hardly eating from worry. Every day he waits for the post man to come. We haven't heard a word from you since you left, only for Ester's Mom, we'd think you were dead. Is that what you want?

He didn't sign his name, or plead with her to write, which led Ester to think that he had done so before. His missives had started with, *please write, Love Bernard* — then *why aren't you writing* — *Bernard*, and finally, *we haven't heard from you since you left.*

Ester told Moire her father was sick. She said she had heard the news from her mother, which wasn't a complete lie. Ester's parents had no phone at home but their neighbors did. Ester rang them to ask if her mother could be brought over and if it was true that Mr. Harding wasn't well. The neighbor said yes, she'd get her mother and to ring back in ten minutes, and yes, Mr. Harding had had been in Sligo hospital for a few days.

Moire had cried in that muddy colored living room, but Ester didn't think it was for Mr. Harding. She was sure it was because of Moire's helplessness. There was nothing she could do in that house. As far as Ester knew she never left it.

"I'm not going back," Moire said.

"Will you write to him?" Ester asked.

Moire shook her head, "I can't."

A press door slammed in the kitchen.

"Didn't you know he was in hospital?" Ester's mother had said, "Didn't he get in touch?"

Ester told her that Moire would not open her letters. She was changing and becoming distant. Ester had cried on the phone and her mother asked her if she wanted to come home.

She said, "London's not for everyone."

"No, I can't leave her now," Ester said.

"She'll be alright," her mother said, "She can get someone else to share the room and she has those other girls for company."

Ester hadn't planned to tell her mother the truth, but she couldn't lie.

It was possible Bernard would have come regardless; it was very likely the worry they suffered in Ireland had started to keep the residents from sleep. Ester could imagine Mr. Harding wandering around in a helpless state, his great bulk diminishing from the dread, until eventually it was decided Bernard would go and see what was happening. But it's possible too that nothing would have been done without Ester's involvement.

"Moire isn't in the flat anymore. She's living with an older man. He's terrible Mammy," Ester said.

"Holy God," her mother exclaimed, "Why didn't you tell us?"

Bernard appeared on a Friday afternoon. Ester's day off, maybe her mother had told him this. Moire had stopped working a few weeks ago. She said she was going to college. She said she had plans but Ester couldn't believe that. She didn't think Moire left the house.

Ester opened her door to a pale, red-eyed Bernard. His jeans and sweater were crumpled.

"What are you doing here?" she asked.

He said her mother had come to their house. He said Moire's father was worried sick, but he was too weak to travel. "It's his heart," he said, and paused before asking, "Where is she?"

Ester wasn't able to tell him. She moved back from the doorway, and Bernard became upset. He asked if she could understand what it was like to hear nothing from Moire, and then to know that it was worse than they had imagined. Moire was being influenced and he had to help her. He couldn't do it without Ester. He was still talking when she appeared in her coat.

Puzzlement crossed his face when she said, "I'm going out now and you better not follow me."

By the time, she'd closed the flat door, he understood.

He didn't sit beside her on the bus, as if she might forget about his presence when everything else paled in comparison. Ester was glad she didn't have to converse, that he wasn't asking questions about Ron or Moire's life here. For the first time in months, she felt relief. The responsibility for Moire was no longer solely hers.

Bernard got off the bus with her, and lingered behind. Every now and again, she'd glance back to look at him. His blond hair was bright amidst the surrounding grey.

At the corner of Lymington Avenue, she stopped.

"It's number 30," she told Bernard and was starting to go when he put a hand on her arm.

"She might feel bullied if it's the two of us," he said and Ester felt stupid for not thinking that herself. "I'll wait here," she said.

He told her, "No, she might see you. I don't want to risk it."

When he smiled, Ester saw the worry in his blue eyes. "I'll only get one chance at this," he said.

A child shouted from one of the houses. Ester hadn't realized how jumpy she was. He asked her to go home, "I'll bring her there." When she didn't move, he said, "Please Ester, I love her."

He started for the house, and then stopped to look back at Ester. She smiled and walked away.

At home, Ester envisioned Moire opening the door to Bernard and crying with relief. She imagined Bernard telling Ron that he was taking Moire home where she belonged. Moire would leave without bothering to pack a bag. And while Ester lay on her bed listening to her flat mates chatter and giggle, they were on her way to her. But as the day darkened, she grew scared that Ron had answered the door and had stopped Bernard from entering.

The lights were off in the living room when the door-bell rang. Ester ran to answer it. Her smile faded when she saw Bernard. He looked as if he'd been crying.

He said, "I don't know what happened."

"You're cut," she said, and reached out automatically but he flinched and her hand fell. She felt like a vacuum had opened between them. The scratch near his eye looked deep.

"What did you do?" Ester said.

She imagined him trying to get into the house and it frightened her. But in the next second his upset became leveled against her. He was glaring when he said, "What do you mean what did I do? I wasn't the one who waited to get in touch."

"I'm sorry," Ester said. "I didn't know how to help her."

He told her it was too late for him to do anything now. He said it was awful. Moire had shouted at him to go away. She said she hated him and wouldn't go anywhere with him. He grew morose when he said he had no choice but to leave Moire in that house.

Ester had spent the day waiting for Moire and Bernard's arrival. Moire was supposed to share her room with her again. They were supposed to laugh at Moire's stupidity while Bernard slept on the couch. Ester had gotten the spare blankets ready for him, but she knew he had no intention of coming in. "It's no use," he said. Ester asked what he was going to do and he said he wasn't staying in this city any longer. She was still standing at the door when he walked away.

For two days, Ester rang in sick. It was impossible to smile and serve customers when Bernard's blame was fresh. She cried in her bed and locked her bedroom door to her flat-mates. The thought of returning to Woodgreen made her nauseous, but on the third day she made the journey. Disembarking from the bus on High Street, Ester remembered how easy it was with Bernard and how nice it was to have someone with her as she trudged through the streets.

She didn't expect Ron to be at home, but he answered the door.

He looked at her for a long time, before asking, "What?"

"Is Moire here?'

"No," he said, though Moire's dark coat was hanging on the peg behind him. Ester glanced at it, but he didn't notice or didn't care. He was about to close the door, and Ester's hand went out. She noticed the cracked and chipped wood on the inside of the door by the latch.

"Her step brother did that," Ron said.

The scorn in his voice made Ester grow limp. She hated his conceit and the way he looked at her, as if she was insignificant. She thought he must have looked at Bernard like that before the door was closed in his face.

For the next months during her journeys to Woodgreen Ester stopped noticing the people in the streets or the stores she passed. With the cushioned seat and the cool glass against her forehead, she thought only of the red bricked house that held her friend. She often felt hollow with the thought of knocking on the door.

Sometimes Ron answered, sometimes no one. Ester would call to her friend through the letter box. "I'm sorry," she'd cry, "I didn't mean to make it worse."

After each failed visit, Ester swore she would not try again. She would forget Moire, but by the end of the week she'd be pulled towards the house. Eventually Moire appeared at the door. She didn't look good with her pale skin and short hair. She seemed tired and unsteady. Dressed in dark pants and a white blouse, she looked light enough to blow away, yet her stare was unyielding and added some weight to the image.

There was the likelihood that Moire would have closed the door in Ester's face, if Moire had not been overcome with sickness. She ran up to the bathroom, leaving Ester at the door. Seconds revealed no other sounds in the house, Ron was not there. Ester closed the door and followed her friend to see her on her knees at the toilet. It didn't occur to Ester at once. There was the rising from the floor, the washing of Moire's face, and the quiet walk downstairs with Ester at her heels. In the kitchen, Moire put on the kettle.

"What do you want?" she asked Ester. "Why do you keep coming back?"

Moire's skin was like putty. She looked queasy. "Oh my God, you're pregnant," Ester said.

Moire didn't deny it. She didn't say yes either.

She faced Ester and said, "It doesn't matter, I'm not keeping it."

"What are you talking about?" Ester asked.

Moire moved past Ester, who followed, though her limbs felt heavy. "But you love Ron?" She said.

"It's not what you think." Moire said. She sat on the armchair. Ester wasn't offered a seat though she wouldn't have been able to take one regardless. Looking into Moire's misty eyes and seeing the paleness of complexion, she was struck with the idea that Moire might break into little pieces if she touched her.

"Then why don't you tell me what it is, what's happening. Jesus you wouldn't have even told me you were pregnant if I hadn't guessed."

"Because you're so trustworthy, how do I know you aren't going to run back and tell everyone?" Moire said.

"I had to talk to someone. I was scared, I still am," Ester said.

Moire's dark eyes fixed on Ester. Moire would give nothing away, and her absence made tears come to Ester.

Ester said, "I didn't know what to do."

"Who said you had to do anything?" Moire asked.

"I should just leave you alone in this house?" Ester asked.

"I was happy," Moire said.

"You were, but you're not now. Help me, tell me what I should do," Ester said.

"Nothing Ester, I want you to do nothing, do you understand!"

There was no music in the house. The curtains were drawn and the air was oppressive.

Ester eventually said, "Ron doesn't want the baby, does he?"

"Ron will do whatever I want," Moire told her.

Ester wondered if Moire really believed that. This woman who had let age creep up before time and had grown cold sitting before the fire.

"Then keep your child," Ester said.

"I hate this child!"

"What's happened to you?" Ester cried.

"I've never pretended to be someone I'm not, I am not the liar," Moire told her.

Ester might have known at that moment that she was going to leave London, though she couldn't remember thinking anything when she left Moire. There was only the slowness of her steps and her desire to lie down and cry.

Ester hadn't been in London a year, before her mother collected her from the bus station. Her mother was a stout woman. Her mouth was tight and hard, the lines crawling through her forehead showed her anger even before Ester heard it in her voice.

"What's this I am hearing about Moire?" Her mother asked. "She won't let her own family visit."

"I don't know what's happening Mammy," Ester lied, "I haven't seen her."

Within weeks at home, Ester got a job in a newsagent on Wine Street a few yards from the bus stop. Most days, she suffered some nausea from expecting to see Moire arrive with her backpack on her back and a shy smile.

Instead, Pete came in. She sold him cigarettes and he asked if he could meet her after work. He said, "I teach in Summerhill."

"Is that supposed to be a recommendation?" she said, though it was easy to picture his tall frame among a crowd of boys and his smiling face gaining trust.

Pete was the only person Ester cried with, the one person she could trust not to keep an account of her talk. He fought against her going to England. "Moire will only hurt you again. Don't do it to yourself." But Ester had counted the weeks to the birth, and needed to see if Moire had allowed the baby to bring her back from the dark place she had disappeared to.

Pete flew to England with her, but she went to that house alone. The moment the front door opened, Ester noticed Moire's small belly.

Moire's smile was kind but her, "Hello Ester," sounded flat.

"Where have you been?" Moire asked, and Ester told her she'd moved home.

Moire said, "Good," and this annoyed Ester. She didn't come for Moire's approval.

Ester scanned the sitting room for a crib or small vests.

"There's no baby here," Moire said. She was standing by the living room window, dressed in dark trousers and a pale pink T-shirt. Her hair was pulled back. She looked tired. Although her gaze was soft, her voice had grown impatient. "Is that why you came?" she asked.

Ester nodded.

"I gave birth two weeks ago." Moire's dead pan voice made Ester feel faint. "I was given this so I might never forget." Moire pulled up her T-shirt to reveal a scar running from below her breast to the button of her pants. Minutes later, Ester ran down through the streets to the park where Pete was waiting, and she was never so glad to have someone's arms around her. She didn't tell Pete about the scar or that Moire said her baby was in a good place. Ron had made sure the adoptive parents were Irish. Ester had resisted the urge to spit with the sound of his name, and had stumbled out the front door while Moire remained standing stiff in the living room.

"Moire wouldn't dare show her face," Pete said when Ester was writing out invitations for their wedding the following summer. He was right. After the ceremony Ester stood under the greenery of Benbulben Mountain sparkling in the afternoon sun. Specks of white clouds drifted by and Pete squeezed Ester's hand and told her, "You have me now."

Moire scared Pete for the hurt she'd caused Ester, but he didn't stop her from trying to write after their first son was born. She sat at the table with the blank paper, and wrote 'Dear Moire.' Then she thought of the baby Moire had given up for adoption. Maybe it was a boy too. He would have been around four. Ester wondered if Moire thought of her child, and if she missed what she had given up. If so, it would be difficult to open a letter only to read 'I have a son' and to write with that news could easily be construed as vindictive. Ester threw the paper in the bin.

Throughout the years, she would try to write several times. There were two more sons and many birthdays passing by, but she never knew how to start. 'How are you?' seemed wrong and 'I miss you' brought her heart into the open. When Pete had his stroke, Ester's eldest boy was twenty and it was like a double suffering, to see her husband pale in hospital and to remember sitting with Moire in Trafalgar Square, whispering about people's lives. It's never as you imagine it, she'd wanted to tell Moire when Pete couldn't work and they'd had to move to the council house on the other side of town. Ester never thought she would get used to the houses built close together and the lack of space, but she quickly made friends with the women in the estate and grew to love the small house and the view of the green where children played.

On a warm September day, she was in her kitchen having tea and looking out at the empty scene when the phone rang. Pete was fishing by the river and the boys were long gone. Two had given her four grandchildren between them. She rose slowly. She was sixty-three and she thought it might be one of her friends from the estate. They would phone again if she didn't make it on time. They knew she didn't like to rush.

She said hello and was asked, "Is this Ester Raines?"

Ester said yes, and heard, "I'm Moire Harding's daughter."

"Oh," Ester said. She couldn't speak. All her grief for her friend had unraveled with the girl's voice.

"I know," she said and Ester heard an intake of breath, "You were her best friend."

Ester's trembling settled a little, though her face was a mess of tears. Her voice was low and shaky when she said, "Where are you?"

"In Dublin," and Ester thought of course. She'd heard the accent. "I only found out about my mother recently, and it took a while to get her address. A man called Bernard gave me your number." She paused and the silence scared Ester. She didn't want this girl to go.

The girl said. "Can I see you?"

"Yes," Ester said, "Please come."

She gave Moire's daughter her address, and the daughter said she was leaving right this minute.

The daughter had waited forty years to find her mother and was two years too late. A weak heart had run in Moire's family. Ron had written after Moire died and the letter had taken a week to get to Ester.

I miss her every day, and she missed you. She wanted me to tell you she was sorry but there were some things she could not tell you. I think she regretted that decision.

Pete had come home to Ester sobbing in bed with the letter still in her hands and had spent the night holding her.

The house seemed too quiet now. Moire's daughter would take at least three hours to arrive. In the kitchen Ester finished her tea while staring out the window. The radio was on and she listened without hearing anything. The D.J was still talking unheard when she took everything out of the fridge and cleaned the shelves and put all the food back again.

After lunch, she found herself stripping her bed. She stripped her boys' beds too, though they hadn't been slept in for months. The sheets were piled up and brought to the laundry. She vacuumed the rooms, and had to search for the dirt and dust.

She started on the bathroom. The lemon scent from the detergent was a comfort to her. She was on her knees by the side of the bath and scrubbing the rim when the doorbell rang. It took longer than she would have liked to stand. She ran to the front door. When she saw Moire's daughter, the ground shifted under her feet. Without the door for support she might have fallen. The girl was tall and slim with straight brown hair, but her eyes frightened Ester. She'd seen those blue eyes so many times before, and it was hard to stand with the rush of memories that ran through her. She saw Bernard at Moire's bedroom door watching with those same eyes, and remembered Moire's upset when she noticed the love hearts on Ester's page. 'You can't like him,' she'd said and Ester never asked why.

Moire's daughter said hello. Ester tried to hide her shock. She said, "Look at me just standing like a fool." The girl laughed and Ester remembered the cut on Bernard's face and the cracked wood on Moire's front door. She must have tried to stop him from entering. "I was happy," Moire had said.

She was until Ester led Bernard to Woodgreen, and Ester realized that Moire had always been trying to escape him. Tears came to Ester's eyes. She said, "I'm so glad you're here."

Moire's daughter nodded and there was something in her movements that reminded Ester of Moire, a nervous shuffle of her feet, the slight bend of her head. Ester stepped back to let her enter. She might have been thinking of second chances then, or maybe that came later.

Blackbirds

IT'S NOT LIKE I spent years thinking about Hagan. I didn't give a damn about her when I lived in Dublin and I don't remember thinking of her when I was in secondary school. I dropped out at fourteen anyway. It was always crap and I was hardly ever there. But I waited around a couple of years for Joe to finish. He was the smart one and funny. He always made a joke of everything. Joe wanted to be a musician. I just wanted to get away and after five years in Dublin, Joe was dead and I was back.

Hagan was my first teacher. When I started school, there were hardly any kids in the village so there were only two teachers. She had the younger kids, from 5-8. We were all in the same classroom. It's changed since then. There are more houses going up, but back in the day Hagan never had more than fifteen kids in the room. She was constantly moving around the classroom giving exercises and orders. Joe said she must be dizzy. He tried to make me laugh, but I never found anything funny about Hagan. She took a disliking to me straight away. One of the first days in school, she pointed at letters on the board and asked me what they were. I refused to answer. I kept my mouth fastened and every time she prodded me, I shook my head harder.

I was nine when the other teacher Richmond said I had dyslexia. At that stage I couldn't give a fuck. Hagan had decided I was a trouble maker years before. I'd spent hours in the corner of her class room. My legs would seize up from standing so long. I never said anything to Ma. Ma didn't talk much anyway. As for Dad, he was a long haul truck driver, he probably still is. I don't fucking know. He stopped coming home when I was 7. But I don't really want to talk about school or my parents or any of that crap. I just want you to see the type of person Hagan was. So you can understand everything that happened.

After Joe's funeral, I couldn't go back to Dublin. Weeks were spent in my room staring at the walls until Ma's friend, Faith Wheeler, came to the house to ask me to wash dishes for her. Faith wasn't so bad. She was small with dark hair and lively blue eyes. Everyone else had a dull disinterested gaze. My last boss in Dublin was like that. He was a mechanic and I was his apprentice. He used to tell me things and all I could see were his dead eyes peeking out from the dirty face. Half the time I wouldn't listen and his voice would rise as if that would make a difference. After I got the sack, he refused to pay me for the week he owed. He told me to get lost, so I did. But down the road, I started to think that it wasn't right that he was keeping my money. I went back. The garage was empty and I spotted the tool box lying off to side. I went for it without thinking that the boss was in the jacks and would be done before I could get away. Joe was on his way to the police station when the accident happened. I don't really like to think about that, or how strange he looked at the wake. I stood at the coffin for a long time, and he was nothing like the Joe I knew. He wasn't there. I might have believed that if it weren't for all the crying and sniffling. People were coming up beside me blowing their nose and saying it was so sad, and I couldn't look at their faces. I wanted to disappear into the coffin with Joe. I wanted to be invisible. His mother kept coming in and out of the room. She'd sit for a while and then start bawling. She'd always made me nervous. She had a way of looking at you as if she could see deep inside and she didn't like what she saw. I was too preoccupied with Joe to worry when she came beside me. I wasn't expecting her to say anything.

"He was on his way to you, wasn't he?" She said. She waited for me to say something, but I couldn't. I couldn't even nod.

After the funeral, when Ma told me there was someone downstairs, I was sure it was Joe's dad. He was too drunk at the funeral to do anything but sit at the table, and I'd been waiting for him to come see me. I didn't think of avoiding the beating, anything was better than the buzzing in my head. I went into the kitchen and instead of Joe's dad, I saw Faith. I don't know why I didn't turn around and leave straight away. It might have been the way Faith was looking at me. It reminded me of Joe. She didn't look uncomfortable. She looked on the verge of some joke and I was curious. Then she said she really needed my help. She asked if I could come in for a few hours a day to chop vegetables and wash dishes. Ma said, "Come on Lou, it's been six weeks, you need to do something." The idea of six weeks was shocking but it wasn't at the same time, like passing a car accident you know is never going to touch you. Faith probably took my silence as me being shy or something, because she said that I didn't have to see anyone, I'd be in the kitchen all the time. And then I was nodding. I thought it might be good to get out of the house and earn some money, and I liked the idea of not seeing anyone. But Faith wasn't right about that. I could see people coming and going even if they couldn't see me, and who did I see, only Hagan.

The café's kitchen window looked out to the field and a new housing estate that was being built. Station road led to the housing estate. When I was a kid I cycled that road a few times looking for Hagan's house with a rock in my bag. I'd been dying to break her window, but I could never tell which house was hers. She didn't drive a car. Every day she walked to and from school.

Eventually I gave up and I didn't remember any of this until I heard her say, "I'm in a bit of a rush." There was no mistaking that deep voice. For a second I was sure she was right behind me, glaring over my shoulder like she used to. I managed to turn around.

Late afternoon, the café was empty. The front door was directly opposite the kitchen. Only three tables separated me from Hagan. She wasn't tall. I could see her coat, but Faith was blocking her face and I felt a cold surge of excitement like when I saw the tool box, only it was different too because there was no panic or rush. I stayed still and watched Hagan walk away. I got a glimpse of her figure in the wool coat and black hat. Her cheeks had gotten fat. Faith was walking towards me. "Poor thing," Faith said, "She must be lonely."

I wanted to laugh but the sight of Hagan had dried me up.

I said, "She lives on Station road right?"

Faith said, "Yeah, I was so sad when she stopped growing her roses. I loved them as a child. Still I can't blame her."

I didn't know what she meant. All I could think of was those roses. They were yellow and red and they'd thrown me off. Years ago when I looked for Hagan's house, I'd never thought the bright home at the end of the row of cottages might be hers.

We finished work at 7 and left the café together. I took out my cigarettes while Faith locked up. Her car was parked outside the butcher's. On the other side of the road was Spar supermarket, and Joanne's hairdressers. I smoked and waited until Faith drove off. Then I started for Hagan's house and for the first time in months, I felt close to happy.

The house was ablaze with lights. I was afraid Hagan would recognize me at the door. I was as skinny as ever and not too tall. I had a nose ring. My hair was cut short instead of long like it used to be. But I hadn't changed too much.

There was no car in the driveway but that didn't mean anything. She probably never learned to drive. The glass by the front door was the distorted bubble kind. I rang the bell.

My mouth was dry and tasted like steel. I planned to push my way in as soon as she opened the door. I didn't want to give her a chance to look at me. Even if she didn't recognize me, she'd see enough on my face to worry her. The thought of her sickened me so much. She didn't answer the door. If the car hadn't passed I might have stayed longer, but I was sure it slowed down a little and whoever was driving was watching me. The silence got to me then. It was cold too. My fingers were numb. It wasn't until I walked the mile home and was lying on my bed that I realized I could have gone around the back and broken in. I'd done it before. The first house I broke into was a student house with a flimsy back door. I knew that because we gate crashed a party one night. It was the most boring party I've ever been to. Still it was worth it because I found out the students were all going home for Christmas. I went there with a screw driver ready to take the lock apart, though I didn't need it, the handle was so loose. It wasn't a tidy break-in. The door frame got badly chipped. I did better with the second house.

I thought of going out again. My dad's tools were probably still in the shed, but I didn't want to see Ma. I'd tried to ignore her earlier. She'd followed me down the hall, calling after me, Lou, Lou. Her voice made my head ring. I told her I wasn't well and just wanted to go to bed. She was still in the hall when I closed my bedroom door. I didn't feel like dealing with her again. So there was nothing I could do but wait. At some stage I fell asleep, but I dreamed of the blackbirds and there was no more sleep after that.

The blackbirds were in the old graveyard at the back of our housing estate. Me and Joe used to smoke there whenever Joe managed to steal cigarettes. All you had to do was cross the overgrown field with the bench that I never saw anyone sit in, and then go down the narrow lane to the graveyard. It was a cool place with old tombs and a really old church with grass growing on the walls. Some of the gravestones you couldn't even read anymore. Joe used to tell me what was on them. The river ran beside the graveyard and there was a waterfall. I used to love watching the water fall over the rocks when I was stoned, but the place was never really the same after we saw the blackbirds. Their cawing was like screams. Joe said they sounded like battle cries, but I thought it sounded like something a lot worse and I was right. The birds were busy feeding on the animal. Their beaks were pecking at a mess of blood. It looked like a cat, but so torn apart by the time we got there, it was hard to know what it was. The eyes were probably the first to go. It still makes me sick to think of it. Joe told me not to be stupid, they couldn't have done that to a cat, but sometimes he pretended things weren't the way they were. If he was there, he would have told me to forget about Hagan. He would have said that there was no point in getting into trouble again, that Hagan wasn't worth it but he wasn't there.

I thought of Hagan all the next day and had to keep busy. When there were no pots to wash I started cleaning the shelves. It was December, and I watched my reflection appear on the kitchen window. I was getting nervous by 4 pm. My stomach was beginning to turn and my heart was going faster than normal and I had two hours to go.

Outside, I had to wait for Faith to drive off so she wouldn't see me go down Station road. She took her time too. I'd smoked half my cigarette by the time she was gone. I waited for a few more seconds just to make sure, and then, if you can believe it, Hagan came out of Spar.

She was holding a bag in both hands. The weight pulled her down and her face was away from the light, but I would have known that block shape anywhere. I felt like I was stoned; you know when you think you're the only one who's seeing the world properly. I knew exactly what to do. Hagan was walking towards Station Road. The street lights would end at the café corner. Soon she'd fade into darkness. I threw away my butt and stamped on it. I waited. There wasn't any point in going just yet. I didn't want to walk all the way to the house with her and listen to whatever crap she had to say. So I counted to fifty twice in my head. Then I followed her. She hadn't gotten far. It was easy to see her fat body in the lights in the houses. She was slower than she used to be. In one of the bungalows the curtains were open. The television flickered and the living room was filled with an orange glow from the fire.

I picked up speed. Hagan was opposite the entrance of the new estate. I skipped from the pavement to go towards the houses. Then I pretended to notice her. I asked if she needed a hand.

She stopped to study me, but the lights from the houses were weak and I kept my head down. I said my family just moved into the estate and I was on my way home. My voice didn't sound right to me, kind of dry and flat. Being close to her was weirder than I thought it would be. I felt sick. I pointed to the bags and said, "They look heavy." Then I was beside her. I heard her breathing and it was like getting too close to a fire, when you want to jump back, but I didn't. My hands were over hers. She was saying there was no need even as her fingers eased and she let the bag go. I was going for the other bag. I expected her to recognize me, but she just said thank you. She said she was getting tired. She didn't realize how heavy everything would be. She said hers was the last house on the row and asked my name.

I pretended I didn't hear her and said, "It's late to be shopping, isn't it?"

The pulse in my neck was going crazy. Her steps seemed slow. I'd forgotten what I'd asked until she said yes it was late, but she was away all day and she didn't get back until around an hour ago. Then she realized she had nothing in the house. She sighed. The houses were further apart now. She said she couldn't get into the car again. All day she'd been inside and it was good to get out. Then she asked what I was doing out so late. I didn't want to answer. I would have liked to walk in silence and feel her discomfort rise. In my head she was telling me not to stand like that Lou Denison; you look like an eejit, head up. But I told her I was out with a friend.

She said. "How nice." And I thought you're such a fucking liar with your 'how nice' and kind voice. *I know exactly who you are.* The lights were on in her house just like the previous night. For a second I was afraid someone was waiting for her. Then I thought she probably left them on because she didn't like to come back to a dark house. I was worried she'd ask for her bags before we got to the door but she kept going. We reached the front steps and she was rummaging for her keys. My face felt tight and uncomfortable. I was sweating in the cold. With the hall light streaming through the side window I saw her mouth was droopy and tired looking. She'd never seemed tired in the classroom. She'd been quick and relentless. She smiled at me. Her green eyes weren't as fierce as they once were. She'd gotten old and she said, "You can leave the bags right there."

I put the bags down. She was saying how cold it was when the door opened. I asked if she wanted me to carry the bags inside. She said no thanks. She said, "Thanks for your help." And I heard the worry. She must have sensed something odd in my study of her. She glanced at the bags by my feet and I knew what she was planning the second before she darted into the house. I jumped up and caught the door before it closed, and pushed her back. She made a weird noise when she fell on her side.

"Don't move," I said, though I didn't think she could. She was trembling. I grabbed the bags. It wouldn't do to have some-one notice them on her steps and knock. The house smelled like hot milk and stale air. I wanted to gag. There was a closed door to the left, and ahead I saw a kitch-en table. Every light was on and it made me uncomfortable. I asked if there was anyone there. She shook her head. She wasn't crying, but she was heaving as if she was finding it hard to breath. She flinched when I walked past her to look down the hall. That should have made me smile, but I was distracted. There was a strange feel to the place. It didn't feel empty. There were four doors off the hall. All were closed. There was a narrow gap between the door and the floor. Light filled every one. I felt a tingling in my back. I glared at her and said, "Who's here?"

She said nobody. I looked down the hall again, and was sure I saw a shadow behind one of those doors. I wanted to believe it was my imagination. Nothing she said hinted at her having company. When she told me about her day, she'd said *I* was away, and *I* didn't get back until an hour. There was no 'we.' Still I felt light-headed.

The silence was getting to me. I pressed my ear against the living room door and listened for something. I didn't want to go in, but I couldn't take the chance of ignoring the room either. My hands were sweaty when I turned the handle. There was a pounding in my ears. The room was bright and empty. The wall had pictures. I was too nervous to look at them. There was no one there. Still I was shaky when I stepped back into the hall.

I'd imagined holding Hagan in the kitchen. She would sit in the chair and I would stand over her so she could feel what it had been like to have her breathing over me as a kid. But I didn't want to go in there yet. I went down on my knees, and I realized I wasn't so angry with her. I mean I hated her, how could I not, but I wasn't so focused. My head was foggy. Her breathing had settled and she was dry-eyed. That didn't surprise me. She probably never cried. Her green eyes had faded in color and there were deep lines on her forehead and around her mouth. Her chin had doubled. I let her search my face, though it made me itch. It was only a matter of time before she recognized me.

Her mouth dropped open. She said, "Lou Denison, oh God."

She started to cry. She said she was so sorry. Not a day went by without regret. Her tears confused me.

She said, "Don't think I haven't suffered." And I tried to laugh but it was a strange sound. Nothing felt right.

She said, "I lost my daughter."

"You didn't have a family Miss Hagan."

Her eyes weren't lifeless, not like I expected. They were sad. When I noticed that I wished I hadn't. I wished I hadn't given her a chance to speak either. I should have hit her straight away, because I couldn't now. It sounds stupid, but I couldn't even stand up. She said her name was Mrs. Neary now. She said, "You must have known, everyone did, maybe you thought I'd brought it on myself. Did you think that I didn't deserve to be a mother?"

I didn't remember hearing anything about it, but maybe I did. Maybe I laughed and said it served her right. I glanced towards the hall. She said there's no one here. Mr. Neary left after the funeral. "He couldn't forgive me. He asked me not to take her out. I was only learning to drive and the roads were so icy."

Outside a car passed. I thought of her neighbors sitting in their cozy living rooms.

I don't know why, but I asked, "Are you afraid of the dark?"

She had to steady herself before telling me, "My daughter was."

She said, "Do you want to see her?" I wanted to say no, I don't want to see your fucking daughter, I wanted to push her back on the floor, but I couldn't. I was standing with her. She was reaching for the living room door. I imagined twisting her arm, but she was so limp and ridiculous, I didn't want to touch her or have her look at me with those sad eyes. My head was roaring when she stepped into the living room and I followed her inside. Above the mantle was a large framed photo of the little girl. She looked around four or five. She had brown hair and green eyes like her mother. She was wearing a white dress and I couldn't take my eyes of her. She was smiling at me, I swear to God she was.

"You're crying," Miss Hagan's voice surprised me. I'd forgotten she was there. I wanted to tell her about Joe. I wanted to say that her daughter reminded me of him, but I was afraid to break the quiet. So I said nothing for a long time.

THE MAN ON SEA ROAD

THE MAN WAS AVERAGE height with sloping shoulders and a round belly. His hair was plastered against his head from the rain and he had to pause to wipe the drops from his glasses. He wore a rain jacket and had a bag on his back. The waitress and the sole customer sitting at the table by the window noticed that he appeared flustered and unsettled as if it had not been his intention to go into the café and now that he was here, he wasn't sure what to do. His age was hard to determine. He had the soft swelling body of middle age, but from where the woman sat she could see no distinct lines on his face. She hadn't been so lucky. Her skin was ravaged with wrinkles, but she liked to think there was dignity in her ruin. She was dressed in a smart navy suit and sat straight backed and confident.

A couple of hours ago, a man had phoned her to ask about the house on Sea Road. His voice had been soft but urgent with his need to meet her today. It never occurred to her that this was not the man. She had lived in the small town her whole life and knew everyone. She had never seen him before. He walked to her without hurry or any particular ease. In his shuffle, he appeared self-conscious and a little nervous. The young girl working behind the counter was watching everything closely. It was 3pm and the place had the feel of late evening. The rain brought a gloom on the interior of the café sending shadows over yellow walls and wooden tables.

"Mrs. Henderson," he said, and she told him yes that was she. The bag was placed on the floor and he sat opposite her without taking off his jacket. She saw that he was at least fifty. His skin was pasty and pale. Extra flesh had gathered around his cheeks and jaws, and the eyes behind the glasses were tired and a little red.

The girl was beside them and he ordered a black coffee with barely a glance her way. A radio played in the background. The music was so low it was impossible to make out the words. The smell of grease and fried food still lingered after the lunch crowd. It was the only place to meet in town with exception to the dark pubs and Mrs. Henderson would not have met a stranger there, though she was sure it would have suited this man better. He looked shaken.

"You haven't said your name," she said. He nodded, and took a moment too long before saying William. The utterance sounded like a question, as if he was sounding it out for the first time and was unsure of the name's suitability. She was convinced the man was lying and would have hated him for it, if he hadn't appeared so uncomfortable with the deceit. He was not a practiced fibber and she should have known. She'd been married to a superlative liar for forty years. She might have questioned him, only he seemed nervous enough and she didn't want to alarm him and make him leave. Now that she'd driven the fifteen minutes to town she was in no rush to go back to her large silent house. Plus she was curious about him with his soft hands and glasses and the sorrow on his face. He seemed like a fifty year old boy.

She asked how he'd found out about the house, and he eased a little as he told her he'd taken the Sea Road out of curiosity. She said nothing about it being a strange day to go exploring, and let him explain that he'd overlooked the house first. He'd driven by without a glance and was surprised to see it on his way back. It seemed impossible that he could have missed the place. He'd stopped the car because for a moment he was afraid that he'd taken a wrong turn, but of course there was only one road to and from the sea. He'd seen the sign in the window then.

It must have been six months since she'd put the For Rent sign up in the living room. Her daughter had laughed, "Who'll see it Mammy?"

She wondered what she would say to her daughter about this man.

"Are you working around here?" she asked, and he shook his head. She expected him to say something but he remained silent. He seemed hardly aware of her as he glanced out the window. The streets were grey from the rain and people hurried by huddled in their coats. They were in a small town built on a hill in Donegal. She imagined he'd driven some distance to get here. On the phone she'd thought she'd heard a tinge of a Dublin accent.

His hands lay tucked under the table. He had not touched the coffee that had been set on the table in front of him. Nor had he said thank you to the girl when she'd left it there. He seemed shivery and cold, but when she asked him if he was okay he said he was fine, just tired. He'd been driving most of the day.

"From where?" she said, and he regarded her for a moment before saying the name of a town unfamiliar to her. "It's in Sligo," he said, "On the Dublin side."

"So you're on holiday?" she said, and he said not exactly. Even with his strange behavior she didn't feel threatened or uncomfortable. She knew what it was like to have the ground pulled from under her, and had no doubt he'd experienced something like that. It was the lack of energy that told her and the way he sat slumped in his seat. She imagined his wife had had an affair. Maybe he'd found the lovers last night and had spent the night in the car, which would account for his tired eyes.

He told Mrs. Henderson that he really liked the house and the location. He said he was a man she could trust. He'd take care of the place. Mrs. Henderson let him finish, though she'd already decided to rent the house to him for at least a few days. No one had stayed there for two years and it was only standing idle. This man needed to rest and it would worry her to think of him driving. Besides, she didn't have the will to argue with him. It was easy to imagine him grasping her hand and pleading with her to let him stay. There would be a scene, and Una Walsh's daughter with her greasy hair and acne would have the town told in a day about Mrs. Henderson and the stranger. Some would probably think this man had something to do with her lying husband. If there had been other women, why not children?

"How long do you want the house for?" she asked. She had expected him to say a week, but he surprised her by saying a year, maybe more. The gloom seemed to drift onto the table and she saw him with different eyes. The boyish innocence was not nearly as prevalent as the nervous worry. Maybe he'd done something. He might be using the house to hide away. "You trust too easily," her daughter had said. "How did you have no idea?"

Mrs. Henderson leaned across the table. Una's daughter was watching them closely and without disguise. She'd rested her elbows on the counter. In another hour, the school kids would swarm in to drink coffee and smoke. The place would become something different altogether and not the scene for an old woman and a strange man to converse in whispers.

"I'm not very comfortable with all this," she said, "I have no idea who you are and I'm pretty sure you're name isn't William."

He seemed embarrassed, but his lack of denial eased her a little. Finally he said, "It wasn't a complete lie. William is my second name. My first name's John."

"But you've been called John up to now."

He nodded and dropped his gaze. His hand was on the mug and his finger ran up and down the sides as if it was a face he loved. "I lost my daughter," he said.

The silence issued between them, though it was not entirely uncomfortable. They didn't look like strangers. The girl watching them thought that he might be a nephew that Mrs. Henderson hadn't seen in a while. Maybe the man had come with bad news from the family. Mrs. Henderson wasn't as upset as he was, though she was used to bad news. Everyone knew of the woman from a few towns over who came to the husband's funeral. "I'm sorry." Mrs. Henderson said.

He said, "Have you ever wanted to disappear?"

"I'm sure everyone has, but it's another thing to do it."

He nodded, and said he knew that but he needed to get away for a while. "I have I.D, you can run a check." He picked up his bag and she noticed his wedding ring. A chill ran through her with the thought of a woman alone somewhere. "Does your wife know where you are?"

He was looking in his bag when he said "No, my wife doesn't know where I am. I'd prefer to keep it that way."

Mrs. Henderson didn't know what to say. She was tempted to get up and leave but he looked so pitiful. He could hardly look at her when he said, "There were reports, not many, just one or two, but that should have been enough, shouldn't it?"

Outside a body brushed against the window. There was laughter but Mrs. Henderson couldn't take her eyes off the man. His eyes were terribly sad. He didn't look away when he said that his wife was a primary school teacher. A couple of her students had been treated badly. They had gone to the next class in a bad way.

"They were afraid the other teacher said. Richmond his name was. I met him a few times. He was the nervous kind. I thought that was the problem that he was getting panicky over everything and I wouldn't believe him. The complaints were never made official."

Mrs. Henderson felt weary.

"After my daughter's accident with just the two of us in the house I kept thinking about those other children." He put the passport on the table and she stared at it for a moment before she realized she was meant to pick it up. The photo inside was of a younger man. He wore the same glasses and his hair cut was neater. John Neary was the name. The birth date made him fifty two.

He said, "I was a business lecturer in Dublin until seven years ago, then I started in the Sligo Regional. Professor John Neary. You can call the college. They'll tell you that I haven't been to work for two months."

She placed the passport back on the table. The girl had started to sweep the floor. Mrs. Henderson was aware of her presence and the body leaning towards them. The passport probably confused her. She would have had no idea what was happening, a man with a passport and Mrs. Henderson whispering to him. Mrs. Henderson would have enjoyed the scene if she wasn't thinking of the man's wife and daughter.

"You must know," she said. The words were more like an exhale. She hadn't made a conscious decision to speak them. He seemed to understand. He was looking kindly at her when he shook his head. She thought it was a stupid thing for her to say. Of all people she knew that it was impossible to know everything about a person.

"If you need other references I can give you the number of a woman from the area. Faith Wheeler, she runs the café in the village. She's known me for years. You could call her, but I'd prefer if no one knew where I was."

The bag was on his knees and he seemed to hug it close to him.

"When a child dies everything changes," he told her.

"Okay," Mrs. Henderson said. "I'd like the number for that woman."

There were things he didn't think of bringing, a toothbrush, soap, shaving equipment, a book that he had half read and that had been lying face down on the coffee table for months. He stopped off at the chemist's with the house keys in his pocket and bought the toiletries. He didn't think about the book until he was driving on the Sea Road, and he had a brief image of the dark cover. The title was lost to him, as was his simple enjoyment of reading. He doubted he'd ever be able to read like that again. Teaching was the same. After the accident, he'd taken a month off and when the day came to go back to the college he'd been awake all night. Light drifted through the kitchen window amid a sky of different shades of grey and he couldn't move. He'd said nothing to his wife, but he heard her on the phone saying he wasn't fit to come in. "He's not able," she'd said, and he thought of everything else he wasn't able to do.

The house was a small yellow cottage with a bedroom on the second floor. "My mother used to live there," Mrs. Henderson had told him. "She was still climbing the stairs at ninety two."

The mother wasn't gone long, and Mrs. Henderson couldn't bring herself to sell but she hadn't been there for a few weeks. The lawn was overgrown, the driveway gravel. He got out of the car and saw brambles lining the hedge on the other side of the road. In spring, it would be purple with ripened blackberries. He seemed aware of this without forming any thought. It was from memories of other hedges superimposed onto the present one. He had never felt so made up of all his experiences until now. There was something about falling apart that made him remember what it was like to be a kid. He'd sit at the kitchen table with his mother yapping away and refusing to acknowledge the empty chair at the other end of the table. There were evenings running around town looking, yet also frightened for, the sight of his father. He'd left his mother for Dublin as soon as he could. His years in that city had been lonely, though he only seemed to realize that now as he walked to the front door of the house on Sea Road.

Inside, there was the musty smell of neglect. The walls could have done with a lick of paint. He ignored the stairs to his left that led to the bedroom. He was not ready yet for the sight of the bed. He'd left his wife huddled under the blankets. She'd been quiet as he packed.

In the living room, the fireplace held ash and dust. The carpet was the same muddy brown and the window was streaked with dirt. Dark curtains stood heavily at either side. The couch was old and he could already feel the dust in his chest. He didn't care. He was hardly aware of the age of the place, and if he was, it was only with an air of suitability. This was what he needed. This was a house he could disappear into. He was finally alone. He'd brought no photos of his daughter, nothing to remind him of that life he'd had. He thought of her photo on the wall above the fire place in that other house. Her eyes were the same green as her mother's and her face was heart-shaped. Every time he'd looked at that photo he felt as if a hand had clutched his heart and squeezed all the life out of it. He'd wanted to ask his wife "Was she happy?" He'd wanted to tell her that something was happening to his memories. Ever since he'd gotten the phone call at work and was told about the accident it felt as if a mirror had been put in front of him and everything he had believed in had been turned upside down and inside out. But he hadn't asked her because he knew she would say, "Of course she was happy."

The kitchen was at the back of the house. The window looked out on a small garden. There was a round table with two chairs to the side of the sink. The draining board appeared rusty in places. He stood for a long time staring out the window at the field of yellow grass.

"What should we call you?" Mrs. Henderson had said when she came back from phoning Faith.

He'd told her, "William will do fine."

The hedges were sparkling silver from old rain and a patch of blue sky had opened to the East. Around a half a mile down the road William came across a large farm house with a red door and red trimmings on the windows. He'd passed the house in the car but it had seemed uninhabited then. The front walls were shabby and weather beaten. The garden was a mess of wood. Now he saw they were rows of raised beds. A noise came from the large shed towards the back of the house that might have been a saw. The double doors were opened and a dog lying lazily by the entrance started to bark. William heard a man's shout but was moving swiftly down the road before there was any chance of meeting anyone.

There had been a book years ago after his Ph.D., *The Relationship between Offshoring Strategies and Firm Performance.* He'd always wanted to write another one. 'Business Strategies for Morons' but of course he wouldn't call it that. It would be titled, *An Introduction to Business Strategies.* It would be published under William Neary, though he couldn't start it yet. It was impossible to concentrate on anything except the smells and sounds around him.

The Sea Road ended in a lookout to the ocean. The cliff was steep, with a clear drop at least fifteen feet. Water was grey and lazy and gave birth to small waves that died quickly. The shore was rocky and empty of people. Sea gulls cried and he remembered his daughter. He hadn't felt panic when he'd first heard of the accident. That came after he'd run into the hospital. It had been a cold wet day. He'd told his wife not to drive because she was only learning. He said don't go, the child might distract you, and she'd said okay fine, but she must have gone soon after he left for work. Her forehead had a terrible gash and he stopped in his tracks when he saw her face.

"John," his wife had said when he was leaving the bedroom with his bags. "Please don't go."

He might have told her that he'd started to disappear the moment he'd seen her in the hospital.

The following day he drove the two hours to the cemetery, built on the rutted road with overgrown hedges. It was surrounded by high walls. The gate was black and was built inside an iron hoop so you had to step inside in two parts. There were no cars outside the walls. It was getting dark, early February. His wife drove a red Fiat. She said she'd never drive again, but he didn't believe that was true. He could imagine her getting into the car one day without thinking. Whatever made him rise and eat and wash and do things that he had no interest would let her sit behind a driver's wheel again. He didn't get out of the car. There was a photo of his daughter on the gravestone and he told himself that he couldn't bear to see her face but he knew that he was afraid of walking through the gate and finding his wife. He sat for hours outside the high wall, but on his journey home he felt exhausted as if he'd trekked miles.

The days started to get longer. The middle-aged woman in Centra on Main Street said, "Back again, you're becoming a regular." He said he'd be around for a while. He was writing a book. "A novel," she said, and he said nothing as interesting, something for business, and chuckled at her disappointed face.

There were books on the floor in his living room. He'd gone back to his wife's house while she was at school and got his work papers and his computer. He had yet to write a single word.

During his afternoon walk, he saw a figure kneeling by the raised beds outside the farmhouse. It would have been hard to tell if it was a woman or a man if not for the flower patterns on her scarf. From where he stood there was tenderness in the slowness of her movements. She wore a long coat and a woolen hat. The sky above her was a clear blue. The dog came from around the back and stood with his ears raised, watching William. Any minute it would start to bark so William turned abruptly. He'd managed to avoid his neighbors up to now by walking early in the morning and in the evening when most were having their breakfast and tea. He'd planned to keep it that way. His breathing filled his head, but he was sure he heard the woman call to him.

They met during the last days of March. There was a stretch in the evenings but a chill persisted in the air that kept the long coats out. He'd started driving to a beach close by and walking on the strand. He didn't like the thought of passing the farmhouse and the woman who may or may not have called to him. But she appeared in his rearview mirror one afternoon. The glimpse showed a narrow face with pinched cheeks and large bright eyes. A dark hat covered her head. Seconds later her grey coat with large buttons was framed in the driver's window. The man with her was dressed in a long black coat. William saw a flash of his skin before he turned off the engine. They were waiting for William when he got out of the car, and he saw the woman was holding a pie. "You're a hard man to catch," she said. "This is my third pie. I hope you like apple."

"Who doesn't?" He said, and thanked her for the offering. A thrush sang in the distance and the sky was darkening with clouds. "I'm Alison Gillespie, and this is Tom." Tom wasn't as tall as Alison. He was slender with a grey complexion. His cheeks were sprinkled with the beginnings of a white beard and he had a wide jaw and a thin mouth. His cap was pulled over his eyes and gave him the look of a hooligan. He nodded and offered his hand for the shake.

"William Neary." It had gotten easier to lie. He felt a speck of rain on his cheeks and saw no choice but to ask them in for tea. He led the Gillespies through the dark hall to the kitchen at the back. The window was grimy and below it the draining board had dishes drying. Alison sat at the table. She didn't take off her coat or her hat. William put on the kettle and wished the couple would leave him alone, her and her smiling inquisitive face and the husband with his impatience stance looking out the window, as if he had been beckoned here and was waiting to be told the reason why. He was wound up and seemed a man unlikely to sit for long any time of the day.

"Tea of coffee" the reluctant host said. Alison said, "We'll have tea," and Tom said, "What about the shopping?"

There were only a couple of bags but William didn't get a chance to say that before Tom was asking if the car was locked. He went for the door before William had finished saying that it wasn't. The black coat looked wrong on Tom's sprite frame. He could take off flying.

Once he was gone, Alison smiled uneasily and William thought she might apologize for her husband but instead she asked if he liked the place.

"It's great. I love the sea."

"Us too, we'd always talked about moving closer to it."

She was at the small table with her legs outward. It was hard to tell her age. Her eyes had a youthful mocking look but her skin was wrinkled. The husband coming in with the bags had deep wrinkles around his eyes and mouth. He tended to frown and looked older than William. "Thanks just leave them on the floor," William said.

Alison said, "Didn't we Tom?"

"Didn't we what?"

"Always want to move close to the sea."

"Aye," he said.

The kettle was starting to boil. William was going for the pie and Alison said, "No, the pie's for you."

"Are you sure?" He said, and Tom said that they'd had to eat two pies this week already and he couldn't take another bite. Alison seemed embarrassed, but she nodded and agreed that she could get carried away at times. The rain started to fall on the window without making a sound. William found the silence between conversations deep and exhausting. He asked if they were from the area, although he could tell by the thick accent that was hardly the case. Alison smiled and said no. He made tea, while she explained that they'd lived in Derry all their lives, but had come here every year for the summer holidays. They'd always planned to retire by the sea. Their daughter still lived in Derry, but came down with her kids every so often. She had two sons who were a bit of a handful so they'd wanted a house with a lot of space.

The tea was put before them with sugar and milk. Tom had taken the seat beside his wife and taken his cap off to reveal hard blue eyes. His gaze was still and focused when he regarded William, who was leaning against the sink with his mug.

"Where did you hail from?"

William told him he'd taught in Dublin for years and had, like them, decided he'd had enough of the city. He didn't say anything about the town he'd just come from, skipping the seven years he'd lived there. Tom said, "You're young to retire."

William shrugged. He could have said that he was planning to write a book or that he wasn't that young. He'd been teaching for nearly twenty five years. But he had a feeling that no matter what he said Tom Gillespie would find fault with it. "What did you teach?" Alison asked.

"Business."

Tom snorted. "It's not doing too good in this country, is it?" He'd put five spoons of sugar in his tea and took a sip. "They all leave."

"Mark's an engineer," Alison said to him.

"So, it's the same thing, isn't it?"

To William, she said, "Our son is in Australia."

"Our daughter's in Derry though," Tom said, "With the grandkids."

"He knows that," Alison said. William drank his tea and was relieved he'd taken the ring off his finger. He wished he'd taken it off before meeting Mrs. Henderson. She'd visited a few times and seemed preoccupied with his wife. "Will you go back?" she'd asked recently and he'd told her no.

He was sure Alison had glanced to see if he'd been married. A ring might have made her ask about children and he wouldn't have known what to say. He couldn't have denied his daughter but he couldn't have spoken about her either.

"How's your garden going?" he asked. Alison looked grateful, and said it was going really well. She had some potatoes already and had planted spinach, Kale and cauliflower, and onions. Every day she was working on it and it was great to have a reason to get outside. The husband said they had a garden in Derry that would have done just as well.

"It was tiny," she said, "And we had no sea air."

"Aye sea air," he said, with an air of contempt.

"Are you here alone then?" Alison said.

"What does it look like?" Tom said, and she looked at him with her wide eyes, and not a hint of surprise or injury. "I was only asking," she said, and her tone was not so much hard as deliberate and slow, as if Tom was a troublesome child. The idea that she was well able to handle him despite her easy and care-free manner was reinforced when he turned away from her abruptly and said, "So the bitch had her pups."

"I'm sure he doesn't want a dog," Alison said.

Tom ignored his wife. "Our collie went off and got pregnant. We hadn't had a chance to take care of her. Six pups, I can keep two but I need to find a home for the rest."

"No thanks," William said. He didn't have to think about it. He felt sick with the thought of taking care of something. "They'll be drowned," Tom said.

"Tom!" Allison admonished.

"I'm only saying."

"I don't want a dog," William said.

"Is that why you came?" Alison asked.

Tom said, "I came because you asked me to. You made a pie."

Her face had tightened, though she tried to hide the irritation with a smile. William put his empty mug in the sink. The sight of the couple at the table had started to sadden him, like looking at old photos where you hardly recognize yourself. Alison told him about a beach a mile past town that was good for swimming. They took their grandchildren there all the time, and William nodded and said he didn't like to swim much. He didn't trust the water.

"Says the man who moved to the coast," Tom said and no one laughed. The light had faded when they thanked him for the tea and stood to leave.

William was surprised to see Alison the next day. It was a blue sky day, tinged with an end of March chill. She wore the same long coat and scarf but had an orange hat. He'd seen her walking into the driveway from the bedroom window and went downstairs to the front door. He imagined her husband in the shed, ignorant of her ambling alone.

"I hope you don't mind," Alison said when he opened the door. He said no, of course not, and stepped back to let her in. She sat in the same seat as the previous day and didn't fill the silence, while he put the kettle on and took the mugs down. A cat had drifted through the back garden earlier in the morning. He thought of it but didn't mention it. Alison seemed too distracted.

He sat in the seat her husband had been in the previous day and saw that her skin was red and dry from the cold. She took a sip from her tea, before looking at him. Her eyes were gold and tired looking.

"I wanted to apologize for Tom."

"You don't need to."

She didn't seem to hear.

"He's like a bear with a sore tooth. He just misses Derry. He didn't think what the move would mean. He thought he'd still be able to go to the local and meet the boys or see our daughter regular. He's wearing me down, but I wanted you to know he wasn't always so gruff and cantankerous."

She drank some tea and he wanted to tell her that people don't change, that she had just refused to see who he was. After the funeral, his wife had held onto him and cried and said, "I'm so sorry, I didn't mean to." And he was forced to remember everything he'd been told about her, but he said nothing about his wife and let Alison talk about Tom's annoying attempts at carpentry. "First thing in the morning he's up making a racket and I swear to God it's only to drive me mad."

"The noise might be worth it in the long run," William said, and she looked askance at him and laughed.

Alison visited him at least once a week. Sometimes Tom would come with her and sit in the corner with nothing but one-liners and grumbling. But mostly he would drive her and leave to finish some piece of furniture he was making in the shed. During her visits, Alison liked to describe the various ways Tom was wearing her down. His late night wanderings with the dog made her nervous. His continued determination to fix up the house depressed her and the miserliness was shocking, but William noticed when she complained her voice held more amusement than frustration or anger.

"Keep her for as long as you can, I need some peace," Tom would say gruffly before leaving and William imagined him laughing when he was alone. William wondered how the old couple had managed without a third wheel to complain and grumble at. There was innocence to the whole scenario that saddened William, though he refused to look too deeply at the cause, if he did he would have known that the Gillespie's made him think of himself and his wife. They'd forgotten how to be together without their daughter. When Alison asked about William, he told her that there wasn't much to say. He was a retired lecturer from Dublin and had lived alone his whole life. He told her he had never fallen in love because he hadn't met the right one. "It's a pity," Alison said, and he said not really, he was happy and sometimes he believed this to be true.

"They know nothing about my wife," he told Mrs. Henderson during his first weeks, and she made a play of locking her lips and throwing away the key while fully aware that he didn't say 'wife and daughter.' She visited him frequently. She liked to walk with him arm in arm down as far as the farmhouse and back. "They'll be talking about us you know," she'd say laughing whenever she got close to the Gillespie's.

She was in her eighties and had slowed down but her hazel eyes were still lively.

"I told Louise that you can stay in the house as long as you want," she told him one day. He'd met the daughter at her wedding, tall with long curly hair and dark eyes, she'd held his hand and said, "Ah the man on Sea Road."

Clouds hung low in the sky and the kitchen in gloom suited the mood that had descended on William. "Don't frown, it's unbecoming," she said.

"You'll be around for a while yet," he told her and she shrugged and said, "Of course, but it's better to be prepared and thanks would have done nicely."

He laughed and said "Thanks."

She said, "I worry about you alone."

She hadn't mentioned his wife in a long time. He'd thought she had forgotten, but she never did. She had an image of his wife as a small timid woman alone in empty rooms. It hurt to think of it and to see William's face close whenever she mentioned his wife. "Mrs. Neary," she called her sometimes, or 'your wife.'

He'd refused to say her name. "It's been so long," she said and he rose from his seat to get away from the pleading in her eyes. Sometimes she seemed like a girl in the way she looked at him.

"She's forgotten me by now."

Mrs. Henderson gazed at him while he washed his mug, and said, "You know that's not true."

He didn't answer.

Eleven years, Mrs. Henderson had kept Faith's number in her address book by her bed. She'd written it down when she'd gotten home that first day after meeting William. Every now and again, she checked it was still there, frightened that she might have forgotten to write it or only imagined that she had. Her mind wasn't the same as it used to be. She couldn't remember his real name for instance. She was eighty-five and lately she felt a shadow around her and heaviness in her limbs. She didn't mind dying. Her daughter was married happily, and her two grandchildren were ten and eight already. Her mother had died peacefully in her sleep and she suspected she would be lucky to have that too. The only thing that frightened her was her friend.

He was staring out the window and seemed to have forgotten her, or maybe he was thinking of his wife. In any case, he was quiet. The rain had started to fall and the pitter patter eased their silence. The thought of rain had nearly made her stay at home, but she felt a ticking inside her. There was not much time left and she had to broach the subject of his wife one more time. She'd often dreamed that he would break down in her arms and admit his loneliness. He'd say, "Of course, how could I be so stupid," and go to his wife. But she'd never gotten anything more than a blank face. "I thought you hated driving in the rain," he said now and she knew the subject was closed.

Mrs. Henderson didn't die in her sleep. She died on her armchair in the living room. For weeks afterwards, William walked every morning and evening and his computer lay untouched. He'd had two more books published at that stage with moderate success. *The Beginners Guide to Business Strategies*, and *Rising Up, why some business make it and others don't*, both were targeted with first year and second year students in mind. He hoped to write a book for the business man now, "*From Good to Great-The Essential Facts.*"

But Mrs. Henderson's death hit him hard. Often, when he walked he'd see Alison Gillespie's bent figure in the garden and he'd stop to speak to her for a while. In the last years Alison's visits had become more sporadic and Tom had softened with age. His gaze had attained a tender almost nostalgic look, and there were times when he drifted off in the middle of conversation. William had the feeling Alison didn't want to leave him alone and when she spoke of her grandsons who were causing some havoc for her daughter, the worry in her eyes was not completely for them. Not long after Mrs. Henderson's funeral, she started to talk about going back to Derry.

"I should have known he'd get his way in the end," she said, and tried to sound light-hearted.

The 'For Sale' sign was not outside their farmhouse long when the knock came to William's door. It was a bright spring evening with flitting clouds and swaying grass. He was having tea in the kitchen and he rose without hesitation. His first years a knock would have startled him and he would have glanced out a window before answering. But that man, overly cautious and more than a little afraid, had disappeared. That man had not been able to go into his living room without remembering a large portrait of a little girl that hung in another house. As he went to the door, William would not have been able to say when he last thought of his daughter.

He opened the door and the shock knocked the air out of him. His hand tightened on the handle.

"Hello," the woman said, but he couldn't answer. There was a distant urge to close the door but it hardly reached him and he stood rigid and defenseless. The woman before him was small and plump. She was dressed in a navy cardigan and skirt. The dark colors brought out the paleness of her skin. Sallow rings were under her green eyes and stringy grey hair fell to her shoulders.

"Your friend told Faith where you were," she spoke haltingly. She was breathless with nerves, while he'd lost the ability to speak. It was not anger or blame he felt when he saw his wife, none of those things he had imagined all those years of his absence. He could see in her slumped shoulders and tired eyes that she had not lived one day without thinking of her loss and he felt weighted with pity for her. She spoke about days of waiting outside his house, hoping for a glimpse of him and trying to find the courage to get out of the car and he remembered Richmond coming to his house, the thinness of the man, the sweaty hands when he said, "your wife has not been fair."

He remembered his wife standing at the kitchen door, pale and anxious and admitting that she had picked on one or two children. She'd said she could hardly forgive herself. After Eve was born she couldn't imagine how she'd been so cruel. She'd cried and told him she understood if he wanted to leave. But he had forgiven her that day in the house while their daughter slept in another room.

Amends

MY FATHER'S DYING.

I haven't seen him in five years.

I hate him (maybe that should be number 1)

My mother just left my apartment

She made me promise to go home for his birthday.

His birthday is in less than a month.

I look like my mother, but it's my father who is a ghost on my back. He's everywhere, in the sideways glance from a stranger, the laugh on the bus, the shout from a few streets over, the sirens in the middle of the night. Sometimes, I expect to see him walking behind me on the street. I haven't seen him in years and I think if he was walking behind me he'd watch me with a snide smirk on his face. He might nod if I looked at him, but he'd keep moving. We'd have nothing to say to each other.

People looking at us wouldn't think we were related. I have my mother's brown hair and blue eyes. He is dark-haired untidy man with hair on his knuckles.

I've spent years being reminded of my father wherever I look and now he's dying. Mam thinks I don't believe it and she might be right. When I think of my father I don't think of a frail man. He's 6ft and has wide shoulders and arms. He doesn't like being argued with and he hates religion, which is probably why I go to mass every now and again. When he dies, I'll go all the time just to piss him off. I'll pray at him, just to annoy him. It'll be easier to talk to him when he's dead anyway.

I lived on Abbey-gate Street in Galway above a charity shop that sold old clothes. The street was always busy with pedestrians. I loved the constant noise and bustle. It was a lot different from where I grew up off the bay in a small village with nothing but the lapping of water that I had to strain to hear. Mam drove the three hours to me once a month. Today she sat in my tiny kitchen, and said, "It's your father's birthday next month and he wants to see you."

I had to sit down. The living room windows were open and we could hear the mumble from people on the street, the sprinkling of laughter. Usually it's a distraction, but today I could only think of what she said.

Mam was tall and thin. She had aged badly in the last years. Her face was drawn and there were deep lines around her mouth and eyes. She didn't know why I left so quickly and had stopped asking. I was twenty, so no surprise that I should move out, but I had to quit my apprenticeship in plumbing when I came to Galway. I'd done a year and I could be qualified by now. But I had no choice.

Mam drank some tea and asked if I was okay. I said, "Sure yeah." I wasn't though. I think I went white in the face. I'd felt light headed and couldn't believe that after everything that happened, I'd been waiting for some kind of acknowledgment from Dad. Still I didn't know if I would go to see him, and I wouldn't have agreed so quickly if Mam hadn't said that it would probably be Dad's last birthday and then proceeded to cry.

For a while, when Dad was first diagnosed she drove to this flat just to cry. I'd open the door and she'd break down instantaneously. I'd hug her, but after a while I wouldn't know what to do, and still her sobbing would go on. By the time she left, I'd feel exhausted. Today she started and I said, "Okay Mam, please don't. I'll go."

She beamed then, poor Mam. I told her it could only be a short visit, since I had to work at least one night during the weekend. She didn't say anything but I saw her disappointment. She hates that I work in a bar.

From my living room window, I watched her walk away, a thin tall woman with short brown hair and a tendency to look at her feet, and I wrote that list. Though, it should be,

1. Marcus

2. I wish I could hate Dad.

The day Dad caught me and Marcus together, Mam was working in the local shop. She came home that evening to a very still house. I bet she stopped the moment she entered. She would have wondered what was wrong. We were not a family anymore. All those moments we'd shared had been blown apart by the incident in the basement. It was as simple as that.

The next day, I phoned Marcus' house and his mother answered. She told me if I ever phoned again she would press charges. She said, "Marcus has a fractured rib because of you. He doesn't want anyone to know, but I swear to God, you ever phone here again, I'll have the guards on ya."

For a long time, I didn't move from my bed. Outside, it was getting dark. Across the water was Marcus' house but I didn't know if he was there or in hospital. I tried to remember him leaving my house the night before, but I couldn't. All I recalled was my father's red face and the spit that came out of his mouth. And when I'd thought of my father coming home that evening, of having to see him pause inside the door and look at me through heavy-lidded eyes, I was restless with nerves. Mam was peeling spuds. Early November, her refection was already cast on the window. She turned with the thud of my bags on the floor. "Where are you going?" she asked.

I told her Galway, and there was a bus in thirty minutes.

When she asked why, what's happened with you two, I told her to ask him, and the pinch of her mouth told me she had already. It was the same look she'd used all through my childhood when I'd ask her to speak to Dad on my behalf.

Mam tried to convince me to stay. She went on about the apprenticeship and the lack of jobs and the fact that I knew no one in Galway. "

"Do I have to walk to the bus?" I finally said.

I phoned her a few days later. I asked if Dad said anything and there was a long pause before she said no. I bet he came in all dust from the quarry. He showered and sat at the table for dinner and didn't even glance at my empty seat. My mother might have said that she drove me to the bus, and he'd have said, "Pass the potatoes."

Once a month, Mam would come to see me. She never told Dad where she was going. She said he knew though, as if his knowing meant he had brilliant powers of deduction, when she disappeared once a month for half the day, and probably had my number by the phone in the hall.

I stayed in a hostel in Woodquay for a while, then a house in Salthill with some students, and finally my own place in AbbeyGate Street. I was still in Salthill, Mam and me were walking the promenade when she said, "Did you know Marcus Blake is getting married?"

Have you ever seen someone nearly drown, they're out cold and pretty much dead. Then they are being thumped in the chest and given the breath of life. I felt like that, a jolt like I'd been thumped and forced back to life. I managed to say no and ask who he was marrying. Mam glanced at me with her worried blue eyes.

"Bernadette Lavin," she said. And I had an image of the red haired girl. She was so quiet in school, sweet like Mam but a more nervous kind. Mam said, "You and Marcus used to be best friends."

I said, "Don't, alright."

The first time I snuck home was when Mam told me about Marcus's house. He did alright, a job with her father-in-law's construction firm and some land to build on.

I wanted to see his place, and I thought that maybe if I saw him I might stop the car. I'd been getting five night's work in the Blue Note, so I could afford a banjaxed old van. Marcus' house was built on the Galway road, before the bridge that led right towards the village's main street. My house was a mile further on that side, so I didn't have to worry about being seen.

His home was a green bungalow with a sloping lane and a large iron gate. There were no cars outside the first time I went by. Opposite was a field and then the river, and down a little ways was the Cottage bar. I drove into the car park and waited for a while. I was sweating and my heart was like a ticking bomb. I thought of what I wanted to say to Marcus. I wanted to apologize and tell him that I didn't understand what had happened in the basement. And I wanted to ask what he was doing with Bernadette.

He'd been married over a year and I still found it hard to believe. I might have tried to see him when I'd first heard of the wedding, but Marcus lived with his parents and sister in the housing estate. It's a small estate of around forty houses and everyone knows each other. There would be no way of driving through there without his mother knowing.

In that car park, I sat for a long time thinking of Marcus

pretending to be someone else. I wondered if maybe he didn't have to lie. I wanted to ask him if everything he'd felt was gone. I wanted to know if that was possible. It grew dark and my legs were stiff. I started back towards Marcus' house. The light was on in the front room. A black Volkswagen Golf was parked outside the house. I kept driving.

Two times, I did that journey and didn't have the courage to go near his house. The third time, I saw him. I was driving passed his house and he was walking out of the gate. He'd gotten broad and his face was set in a serious way that was unfamiliar.

He'd been a bit of a joker back in the day, restless and impatient, bounding down the stairs and jumping up and down with ideas. He'd wanted to open a nightclub then, but he never settled on anything for long. He could hardly sit still, fiddling with music, or perched on the couch, his hands joined, his foot tapping.

He was the one who said, "I've never seen you with a girl." Then he'd said, "Patrick, do you hear me?"

The man I saw walking out of the house was nothing like the smiling dark eyed boy I remembered. Through the rear-view mirror, I had a view of him walk towards the village. I drove into the cottage pub carpark and waited with my head down for him to pass. He looked taller than I remembered. His dark hair was shaved. When he was parallel to the car, I grew afraid that he would look at me. There was something unforgiving in the set of his face.

I never did that drive again. Soon after, Mam visited and told me that Dad had prostate cancer. "He refused to go to the doctor, you know your father, and now it's too late."

I don't know if I felt anything. I didn't consider going to see him. Although she asked a few times, she wasn't persistent because he would have hated me to see him in hospital.

Then she said, "Your father wants you to come home."

And I thought of doing that journey without having to worry about hiding. I thought of being able to park my van on the main street and it was shocking how much I wanted it and how much it scared me.

"What do you buy a dying man for his birthday?" I asked Denise at work. She was small with dark hair and had a tendency to hit, so I kept my distance before asking. "Jesus, you're going to see him?" She was the only one I talked to about Dad, though I wasn't honest. She thought Dad told me to leave, that Mam knew why, and that I hadn't been near my home town in years. "That's brilliant," she said. She gave me a nudge and said, "Isn't it?"

I said, "I don't know."

She said, "He'll always need socks."

The day I was expected, I phoned Mam from Sally Long's pub. It was an evening with a breeze and a few clouds. The people I saw walking seemed to be in a hurry, it was that kind of day.

"Does he still want me to come?" I asked, and I thought there was a pause of uncertainty before she said, "Yes, we're waiting." She'd warned me to expect a change, but when I drove the N17, passed green field and stone walls, I felt as if it was mere hours since Dad had bounded down the basement stairs and grabbed me by the hair. I don't know what kept me driving forward, if it was hope or curiosity, but soon I was passing Marcus' house. The place was in darkness and it felt like an omen. The Cottage bar had only a few cars in front. For the first time in four years, I saw the Statue of our Lady in the alcove opposite the bridge. She was dressed in a white robe and her gaze was held towards heaven. Mam used to take me there when I was young. Once, I asked why the statue's arms were raised upwards. Mam said, "Because of people like your Dad."

I believed her then, maybe I still do.

Over the bridge, a few cars were parked outside The Dun Maeve hotel. Spar supermarket was closed. My headlights were reflected in the dark window of Faith Wheeler's bakery as I made the turn towards home. The bay sparkled in the moonlight. A half a mile down the road was the turn for my parent's house.

Mam was at the window watching for me. I hadn't turned off the ignition, but she was out the door. She looked thinner as if the house took something off her. I was engulfed with the smell of the sea the moment the car door opened.

"He's in the living room," Mam said. Her hand was on my arm. Her touch was light but I felt that she was steering me in and without her hold I'd be left standing by the car. The house was stifling hot. Gay Byrne's voice was coming from the living room.

Mam said, "Come on," and I let her lead me into the living room. I saw the side of the television, the fire, and then Dad.

His dark hair was streaked with grey. He was pale and so thin his pants looked as if they were standing on their own. He was leaning on a crutch. Regardless of the cancer, he was not a man to sit when his son entered the room. Mam rushed to him and asked. "What are you doing for God Sake?"

"I'm fine Annette," Dad said. She was at his side. Her arm went around his tiny waist. No illness could take away from the calm authority in his gaze.

"Hello Dad," I said, and tried to keep eye contact but it was hard not to look away. There was no warmth in his pale eyes. There might have been surprise but I didn't know if it was because I was there, or because I'd changed. My hair was cut short and I'd put on some weight. He nodded and said. "Patrick."

"You don't have to stand on my account," I said.

Dad said he'd never stood on anyone's account in his life and he wasn't about to start now. He said a man ought to see his son home after four years eye to eye. Then he told Mam to leave him alone. "I'm able to drop into a feckin seat."

He pushed her away with an arm that looked like a child's. "She's driving me nuts," he said, "Do you know she quit her job at the shop. I used to have four hours a day of peace."

"I'd heard she quit alright," I said, "After you were rushed to hospital, wasn't it?"

Dad's eyes narrowed and he asked, "What are you getting at?"

"Nothing," I told him.

"Right," Dad said. His cheeks bones were prominent and his skin was a pasty color, but he was still forceful. The gaze seemed to dare me to pity him. And all that time Mam was hovering around him. "The *Late Late show* is on," he said, and I told him I could see that yes.

His mouth tightened. "Don't be a smartshite," he said.

Ten minutes, I thought, ten minutes and four years and all I got was 'smartshite.' He was looking at the television now.

"Annie Murphy's being interviewed, did you hear about her?"

He didn't wait for an answer, but said, "She was the one who had the bishop's child. He's supported the boy for years. These are the people that the nation is trusting with their souls. Didn't I always tell you that it's a pile of corruption?"

"Yes," I said.

"Alright," Dad said. He refused Mam's help, and gasped as he lowered himself down to the seat. Still it was hard for me to believe Dad was susceptible to pain. His gaze was on Gaybo. He laughed at something that was said. Like that, I was dismissed.

In the kitchen, I said. "That went well."

Mam looked at me with a frown. She said, "How about some tea?" But I couldn't sit in the kitchen and talk as if Dad wasn't in the other room. It felt weird being in the house, like we were trying to be something we weren't. Mam didn't seem surprised when I said I was going to my room. My bedroom hadn't changed. It was a narrow room with a single bed and bedside cabinet. I was surprised there was still a phone on my bedside cabinet and it worked. But I shouldn't have been, Dad wouldn't have set foot in the place and Mam would have kept everything as it was. With the door closed and televised voices rising through the floor boards, I got Marcus Blake's number from directories. I hadn't planned on phoning him, I'd planned to stay a night, have dinner tomorrow and then go. But then I was in my old room and it was impossible not to think of Marcus. I dialed the number without wondering what I might say. Marcus' wife answered the phone. She had a sweet voice. I might have hung up, only for the soft way she said hello. When I asked if Marcus was there she was quiet for a second. I wondered if she knew who I was; maybe they'd seen me outside her house and knew I was at home. They might have been waiting for me to call. Finally she said, "No, he's not here." When she hung up, I felt like I'd missed something.

The doorbell rang the next morning when I was thinking about leaving my room. I heard Mam saying hello father. I thought it was a joke until I heard the visitor ask how Dad was. There was something about his voice I recognized, a soft fluctuation that I'd heard whenever Mam had snuck me to Sunday mass. At least once a month, she'd made an excuse and we'd go to mass in towns nearby. I'd loved going, and watching the priest raise his hands with his white robe swallowing his frame and the boys kneeling beside him ringing the bell to signal something important that I always missed. Each time, I hoped I'd understand it more and I listened like no other child would have, straining forward while Mam shuffled nervously beside me. At communion, I had to watch the congregation line up and imagine the 'Body of Christ' was being put into my mouth. "A thin wafer that dissolves in your tongue," was what Mam had said, and I'd close my eyes and think of it, and hear the soft murmurs of amen over and over. And before the last person had gone up, Mam would tug my jacket sleeve and say, "Come on, we've been gone long enough."

We'd walk through the still cars and for a while I'd hear the flutter of a voice in the background, but then nothing but our shoes shuffling on the pavement and I'd hate that sound for the loneliness of it.

Downstairs, I found our priest in the midst of taking of his jacket. The house was stifling hot. I was going around in a T-shirt and bare feet. Mam was standing beside the priest with a smile. She said, "Patrick this is Father Divine."

I said, "Hello Father, I'd say this is a wasted visit."

Father Divine laughed, "It's not my first."

"Your father invited him," Mam said.

I said, "You're joking right?"

It didn't escape me that the priest wasn't much older than I was. Father Divine had a mop of black hair, a square jaw and kind navy eyes. He said, "Your father has gotten some comfort from our talks."

"Who is there?" Dad said from the living room. I was staring at Mam. She was frowning as if *I'd* lost my head. How could she believe Dad took this seriously? I was the only kid in town not to get my first holy or confirmation. My head was spinning. "Is that true Mam?" I said. "Does Dad get comfort from their talks?"

I saw the doubt in her eyes, but she recovered and said yes.

"Are you mad? This has got to be a joke, his last big laugh."

"Annette. Who is there?" Dad said.

To the priest, I said, "My father might listen. He'll nod every now and again but he'll be laughing every step of the way. He has not an ounce of respect for you or your church."

The priest said that may be so, but he wouldn't turn away from one of his congregation. "He's not one of your congregation. He's not a bloody lost sheep. He's a feckin wolf."

"Patrick, what's gotten into you?' Mam said.

"It's okay; it must be hard to be losing a father," the priest said.

I told him that wasn't it at all.

"For God sake," Dad shouted, "Do I have to go out there myself?"

It occurred to me that the only way to stop the priest was to wrestle him to the floor and sit on him. I might have done it too if Mam hadn't shouted, "Patrick, what the hell are you doing?"

The priest was looking a little worried. I eased my stance, though it was hard not to try grab his arm as he slipped by. It was easy to imagine what Dad would have said, "*The other boy was kneeling on the floor and my son was on the couch with his pants by his ankles. Can you imagine the shock I got, father?*"

"Are you ok?" Mam said.

I didn't answer. I was in the living room. Dad gave me a thin smile and asked what I wanted. Fr. Divine was sitting perched on the couch beside Dad's armchair. I wouldn't have been surprised if they were holding hands. I sat beside the priest. Mam appeared and was hovering inside the door. She'd become an expert hoverer. Dad said he didn't realize we were going to have a party.

I said, "Last night you didn't have much time for the church."

Dad reminded me that last night he was talking about Annie Murphy." To the priest, he said. "She was being interviewed on *The Late Late Show*. The whole thing would make you wonder."

The priest said, "It would, but you shouldn't let one man affect their opinion of the church. It's important to keep an open mind."

"Exactly father, that's what I've always said," I said, "An open mind is key, who are we to judge after all?" I was settling in now, relaxing on the couch. I could nearly believe in our ability to have a civilized conversation, me and Dad, and the priest, as long as I didn't look at Dad.

"But I know it's against the church's preachings so I was wondering and I hope you don't mind me asking, if I'm stepping over the mark just tell me, but what did you think when my father told you I was gay?"

"Oh Jesus Christ," Dad said. The priest paled slightly. Mam came forward and said, "That's enough Patrick."

I looked at her and it hit me like a fist. She must have seen it in the fall of my face. She glanced at Dad, which felt like a double betrayal. It was a glance of acknowledgment, the 'what should we do now' look. I was standing though I didn't know how.

"When did he tell you?" I managed to ask. For a minute I thought she'd deny everything but she said, "Only a few weeks ago. If I knew before I would have said something."

"What did he tell you?" I asked.

Dad said, "That's enough!"

I refused to look at him. Mam said, "He told me about Marcus," she paused and said, "The basement."

My stomach turned. I said, "Did he tell you about the beating?"

"No, I did not!" my father said.

"Why not?" I asked, "Weren't you proud?"

Dad managed to sit forward. He was raging. He was a bull in the chair. "I had nothing to do with that sordid scene. I warned your mother not to ask you back. I told her that you'd cause some kind of trouble. It couldn't be good, the likes of you in the house, but she wouldn't listen and I've had enough of this shite."

"Mr. Lenhihan," The priest said, and was told to mind his own business.

The priest said, "Maybe I should come back another time."

No one answered. I didn't understand how Mam could be so naïve. If Dad didn't want me around there was no way he'd stay quiet about it. He must have asked the priest to visit the second he knew I was coming. *"It's against the churches preachings, isn't it?"* he would have said.

Mam touched my hand but I pulled away. She said sorry. Tears were streaming down her face. I managed a nod. That was all I could give her. I was trembling.

In the hallway, I heard the priest ask Mam if she was okay.

She might have nodded. The priest said something else that I missed. I was putting on my shoes when I heard the door close behind him. It took some effort for me to tie my shoes laces. Mam knocked on my door and I asked her to please leave me alone. I put on my jacket and waited until I heard Mam go downstairs and into the kitchen before I ran down the stairs. "Patrick," she shouted but I didn't answer.

The day was grey. The clouds hung heavy with rain. I didn't want to think too much about what I was doing. I drove slowly. My mouth was dry. I wished I'd stopped to have a drink of water, but there was no stopping now. A few bodies were around the village. Faith Wheeler's pastry menu was out in the pavement. The people around seemed to be going in slow motion. I drove over the bridge, towards the statue of our Lady.

"What would you say now?" I asked and she didn't answer. Of course she didn't, she just kept her head to the sky and her hands reaching upward as if pleading for escape. "Ah come on," she might have been saying, "Enough is enough."

I was on Marcus' road now. The nerves were starting to get to me. The river was dark and thick. It seemed to crawl by my side. Marcus' Iron Gate was open and I liked to think it was fate. His black Volkswagen Golf wasn't there and a red Peugeot was in its place. I got out of the car before I had time to think and rang the doorbell and waited. The door opened finally and there stood Bernadette in all her red-haired glory. She started to smile and say hello, and then she paused for a moment before saying, "Patrick."

I nodded. Her eyes were brighter than I remembered. And

she didn't seem so shy. It might have been the vibrancy of her red hair falling over her shoulders or her open scrutiny, but she seemed different from what I remembered. My heart was a low drum in my chest and my mouth was parched dry. I didn't know where to start. I expected her to ask what I wanted or to call for Marcus, but she didn't. After what felt like forever she said, "Marcus doesn't live here anymore."

She waited for a moment, maybe for some reaction, but I wasn't capable of thinking or feeling much after what happened in the house. I was exhausted all of a sudden. It was only hitting me now and in front of Bernadette Lavin of all people. I should have walked away but I couldn't.

"You're the first person I've told," she said. "But then of course you know the truth already."

Her smile wasn't exactly sad, but mocking, like she was laughing at herself.

"Aren't you going to say something?"

I told her I was sorry and she shrugged as if she didn't believe me or didn't really care.

"He wouldn't talk about what happened with you two and I need to ask, did you hurt him because he tried it on?"

The question surprised and saddened me. I told her no, and I might not have said anything else, if not for the soft way she was watching me and the lingering shock of Dad's lie. *"I'd nothing to do with that sordid scene,"* he'd said, but he had. So I told her, "I hurt him because my father told me to."

I didn't know what I saw on her face, disgust, sympathy or just surprise. She didn't ask why, then or later. She probably knew some things can't be explained. There was my father's face in mine, there were his screams and slaps and then…well that is the moment when the trigger is pulled, only I had no gun, just feet and hands.

White Trout

THE UNCLE CAME INTO the café with his nephew and sat at the table by the large window, Faith served them. We knew she and the uncle had grown up on opposite sides of the village. It was a small place and there was very little we missed. The uncle's family used to live over the bridge. Through the café window Faith would have been able to see the silver sparkle of the railings in the sun or the rain swallowing it whole.

We'd known the uncle since he was a skinny boy with dark brooding eyes and pent up energy from too many ideas in his head. He and his brother used to have us harassed in the housing estate. They were hardly out of nappies when Mrs. Lavin found them washing her husband's car with sponges bigger than themselves and they told her it wouldn't cost extra if she wanted the interior cleaned. In all kinds of weather, we'd be sure to get a knock on the door and find the Hurley brothers looking to earn a pound, as if we'd had any to spare. We knew of their plans to go to London and they might have made something of themselves if their father hadn't died and the mother hadn't taken ill. The younger brother was left to take care of her and the uncle had to go alone. By the time he was leaving, our children had university degrees. They were teachers, lawyers and accountants, yet we had no choice but to send them off on the boats in search of jobs. The brain drain they called it, when it was our hearts drifting away. They'd come home for Christmas, and the uncle would be with them, disheveled and skinny with dirty jeans and calloused hands from the buildings, and a new liking for drink that we tried to ignore. Sunday at mass, shaking hands during the sign of peace, we'd avoid looking at his red eyes and stubble chin.

At his brother's funeral he was clean-shaven and trembling from the want of it. He sat in the same pew as his nephew and sister-in-law and the space between could only be measured in silence. After the mass, from the low stools in her living room we watched the little boy cling to the grieving mother, and in the kitchen saw the uncle drink tea and step outside the back door. He was smoking when Faith found him there and he flinched with her touch on his arm. Above them was a blue sky. A single seagull cawed on his flight towards the sea. She said she was sorry for his loss. He said he'd lost his brother a long time ago and it was his own bloody fault.

"That's not true," she said, when it would have been better to leave the man alone with his heart-ache. "He cared about you."

She stepped back when he threw the cigarette on the ground and stamped on it.

"If I hadn't messed up, he'd be alive right now."

"Oh," she said, "London,"

He said, no, that wasn't it, and she nodded without listening. The back door opened, but people paused inside. There was a tension to the uncle and Faith that no one thought fit to disturb. She said, "Things happens, you can't wish your life away."

The uncle's eyes narrowed. He said he wasn't the one wishing his life away, staying cooped up in a bloody café day and night. He said he wasn't stuck in the past either, talking about fucking London as if that was important now. That wasn't what he'd been meant at all. His brother had stayed out late with him. He'd been tired because of him.

"I might as well have turned the wheel myself," he said, "So don't talk about things happening."

The uncle's explosion exhausted him. His shoulders slumped. He took out a cigarette and was about to light it when Faith walked away and he yanked the cigarette from his mouth. His dark eyes were pleading on her retreating back, but she was gone before he thought of anything to say.

We felt sorry for them then, children whose dreams had gone to ruin.

When Faith was a girl, her café had been a clothes shop. Bright hats with feathers and trims were on display in the window. Faith wasn't able to pass without gazing inside. Her reflection, petite and long-haired with shabby jeans or school uniform, made the merchandise more exotic. The shop was owned by Mrs. Reilly, a tall regal woman with bobbed silver hair and a Northern accent. Eventually, when Faith was thirteen, Mrs. Reilly invited the girl in. There'd been no need for Faith to go into that shop before that. Faith's mother tended towards smocks and long skirts and laughed at the frills and nonsense. The interior of the shop was small and dark. Faith was inclined to stay near the door.

"They're like sweets," Faith told Mrs. Reilly when the latter asked why she was so enthralled with the hats. Mrs. Reilly laughed and said she'd never seen bonbons as big as that before. And Faith said, "No, I mean pastries."

To Mrs. Reilly, she confided her dream of owning a shop with cakes towering in the window. Every time we saw her on the street we thought of the pastries rising like waterfalls and colored like gems. After finishing school, for seven years she worked in the civil service in Dublin and saved her money. On her return home, the grimy cob-webbed O'Reilly window showed her reflection, no taller, but less dream-like and more set in the mouth. It wasn't the shop we'd imagined. In Dublin, there were places like the bakery on Henry Street with sellers crying their wares and crowds every day of the week, and a store on Middle Abbey Street, which was close enough to O'Connell Street and Dublin bridge to have pedestrians strolling by at all hours, but Faith ended up meeting the wrong man and running home to a shop with barely a foot path in front.

The café's building sat alone at the top of Main Street. On her right was the major road for Sligo and on her left the narrow

Station road. Both led onto our only street, but no matter where we started off we had to cross a street to get to the café's island. The shop could be a glitter with color, but none of us would pass on the way to the butchers or the supermarket, and we'd forget about the pastries until we were halfway home.

The cakes didn't sell quick enough. Faith offered sandwiches and soups, and put out a blackboard with her menu for the passing trade on their way to Dublin or the North. The café was small with three rows of two tables between the large window and the counter, but until the bypass was built she employed a waitress and two people in the kitchen to handle the breakfast and lunch trade.

As for her pastries, we saw advertisements in the local paper with pictures of cakes she'd done throughout the years, birthday cakes in the shape of cars or ponies, wedding cakes that were towers of silver icing, cakes for baptism with the white cross in the center, (which would be surprisingly popular) pink layered Easter cakes that rose from the plate like an egg, and many others she'd catalogued. The orders came in and she'd bake in the evening when the café was closed, so it looked as if she was floating away from the world. With the tables and chairs in darkness and a small light burning in the back kitchen, we'd see her standing at the front window watching the village, a silent unyielding witness like the statue of Our Lady that stood on the other side of the bridge. Most of us had passed the grotto nearly every day of our lives and it was reassuring to think that Faith had taken up the responsibility with her, the young and the old minding everything in between.

Faith kept her distance, though she must have wondered if we knew about Dublin. From watching the village, she'd have understood that she didn't need to say something aloud for people to know. There could have been a silent witness to her life in the city where she'd lived in the shabby one bed-room apartment. A bed-sit would have been cheaper and let her save quicker, but to live without a kitchen would have been torture. Before she'd left home, she'd already had the tools of the trade, mixer, whipping siphon, spraying gun to name a few and she'd spent evenings in Dublin experimenting with different ingredients, such as 'avocado creamed like but-ter' for icing on a chocolate cake, natural sweet beets in batter of a sponge cake, parsnips in carrot cake for added spiciness. Each day, she'd have something to bring in to her colleagues in the office, but she never shared her ingredients until *he* sat beside her on the bus. He was broad with fair hair and spar-kling eyes. His face had the ruddy complexion of a farmer and his voice was surprisingly soft and gentle. The accent was hard to place. He told her Wexford and that he had no family. His hands were small and well-kept with square shaped nails. The cake on her knees was the first thing he pointed to and she told him it was a chocolate potato cake. Maybe it was this that endeared him to her; the simple sharing of her secrets that would go on every morning on the bus, or it might have been his enthusiasm to taste the cake when she'd seen the doubt in his eyes. Regardless, after many tastings he asked to see her kitchen "where the magic happened." She took him there, and so their love affair began.

When it ended she tried to recall details of that first bus ride and wonder if there was something in her face or composure that told him she would be easy to fool. How did he know she would not demand reasons for his cancelled dates or his departure from her bed in the early hours of the morning?

"I need to be closer to work," he'd say, and she demurred without a fight. She was twenty-three and he was in his thirties. A lawyer, he never knew when a case would come up and he'd be smothered with it. When his phone was off for two days in a row he'd arrive at her flat full of apologizes and promises to make it up. He'd tell her he had to work hard and make sacrifices for their future. He talked about children. They'd have a son and daughter he said and, once the babies were old enough she would start the bakery she'd always wanted. She baked for him all the time, Angel cake with sponge that melted in his mouth, strawberry trifle with homemade vanilla pudding, apple tarts with a taste of cinnamon, frosted chocolate layer cake that he couldn't stop eating.

They'd had so many dinners and conversations while his real life had been put on silent. He'd had two phones. His wife found his second one in his glove compartment and phoned the only number on it. Faith became haunted by the woman's faltering voice. Not one memory was left unscathed with the notion of his wife's constant presence. She'd sat at the table with them while they ate in dark restaurants. She'd lain between them in bed while they talked and touched. She was a specter that Faith could not get rid of. If Faith didn't want to walk around the city that had been fouled by his lies, if she'd felt deceived and dirty, how could the woman to whom he'd said, 'I do,' survive? The thought of losing so much was terrifying, so Faith moved home and watched us in the dark.

She was not prepared for the uncle and nephew. The uncle kept his head bowed when they slipped quietly into the café and took their seats. They were both dark haired and skinny with long fingers. The uncle's eyes were large; the boy's smaller and more pensive. His gaze was held on the table when the uncle asked, "Is it a ham sandwich you want?"

The bypass had brought a subdued quiet to the village and there was no one working in the café, except the kitchen porter, so Faith had no choice but to serve the uncle herself. He smiled at her and said hello Faith, but she kept her gaze fixed on her notebook and said, "What can I get you?"

The uncle ordered. He didn't take his suit jacket off and looked strained. Behind him was a dry day. A few teenagers were hanging out in front of the Fast Food Restaurant, a mother was trying to drag her two year old into Spar and the boy and uncle looked like a painting in front of the scene. They were so still, the boy with his hands tucked under the table and the uncle watching him with a soft hopelessness.

From the kitchen, Faith heard the uncle's mumbling and nothing from the boy. We knew the boy's mother had not spoken to the uncle while the brother was alive. But it was easy to imagine how the boy would have clung to her until she'd felt smothered and phoned the only other family they had.

They ate their sandwiches quietly. The uncle asked what the boy would like to do next and the boy shrugged. He had yet to look up and reached for his glass of Fanta with his head down. The glass toppled sideways and spilled its contents over the table. The uncle sat rigid staring at the spillage as if was a living thing. When Faith came to help, he smiled sadly at her and she couldn't help nodding back.

The second week wasn't much different, only it was raining and on arrival their hair was sparkled with silver drops. The boy sat in a tight angry ball. The uncle stared out the window when he'd finished his sandwich, not like a man with no interest but one preoccupied with thinking about something to say. He was staring at the street with an intensity that made his eyes narrow. He didn't glance at Faith when she brought the bill and cleared the table, and he might have sat there longer if the boy hadn't said he wanted to go home.

"Do you like stories," the uncle said on the third Saturday. The grey day sent a shadow over them.

"What kind?" the boy said and the uncle shook his head and asked, "What do you mean what kind?"

The boy shrugged and the uncle repeated, "Do you like stories?"

The boy nodded and might have mumbled yes. Faith was at the counter, writing. She kept her head down when the uncle started, "Long ago, in a place called Cong in County Mayo there lived a young woman. She was about to marry the king's son who she loved very much, but he was killed in a fight."

"What kind of fight?" the boy asked. The uncle shrugged and said he wasn't sure, but it was a bad one and everyone in the village was very sorry for the lady. One day she disappeared and the villagers thought that the fairy people had taken her away. Then they noticed a white trout in the lake. This was strange because a white trout had never before been seen in the area.

"Was it her?" the boy asked.

The uncle winked and said that he'd find out soon enough. He said the villagers watched the white trout for many generations and it never changed its appearance or its habits. The people thought the trout must be a magic fish and always treated it with great respect. But a stranger came one day and caught the fish.

The boy's dark eyes had widened. He looked scared. Faith held her pen but had forgotten to keep writing as she listened to the uncle describe the fire the stranger built to cook the fish. The stranger put the fish on a skillet and kept it there over the scalding heat but the trout wouldn't brown. No matter how long it was in the skillet it stayed white. The stranger wasn't too worried. He thought he'd eat it anyway and got his knife and fork.

The uncle paused. The boy was like stone.

"The stranger cut into the fish," the uncle said. "And he heard a loud scream and before him was a beautiful woman. Look what you've done? She says to him. I'm bleeding. And why did you take me out of the lake. I'm waiting for my love, so you need to throw me back in immediately. The stranger said he couldn't throw a beautiful woman back into the lake. She told him he'd better, or she'd haunt him forever and at that she turned back into the white trout. The stranger raced to the lake with her and put her back into the water where there was a stain of red from her cut. And to this day all trout have a red mark on their side."

Ahead, over the bridge was a dense patch of clouds. The boy asked. "Why did she do that?"

He couldn't have been much more than seven but there was a seriousness in his eyes that belonged to an older man.

"Do what?" the uncle asked.

"Wait for him when he died. Doesn't she know he's not coming back?"

"I don't know," the uncle said and his glance towards Faith made her shoulders straightened. Her strides towards the table were quick and urgent. The uncle and nephew were startled when Faith slammed down their bill. To the uncle, she said, "Not all women wish their life away and spend their time waiting."

The nephew stared up at her with the dark eyes. His held surprise and little fear. God, he was a nervous child, and the uncle gazed up at her with soft apology.

"It's just a story," he said.

The lights in Faith's kitchen burned all that night. It was getting bright by the time she had the last cake out of oven. She was first to mass. We noticed her at the top of the church sitting erect with flour in her hair. It wasn't a surprise when the priest made the announcement that there would be a giant cake sale. Faith was barely in the door of the café before we started to arrive. We bought chocolate cake with buttermilk cream; lemon cake with marshmallow frosting, gooey butter cake, bite sized strawberry trifle and Almond honey cake, to name a few. The uncle was among us. It was a warm March day, yet he wore a long coat, and he didn't step into the café. He watched us come and go with pastries hiding our faces and when he saw the nephew arrive hand in hand with his mother, he walked away.

The next week was a clear day with a slight breeze. The morning was slow going. Faith kept glancing at the clock, though we weren't sure what drew her eyes there, until it reached 2.15 and she stood at the counter with a hardened gaze and her attention on the window. The uncle was in his usual suit. Since he'd stopped drinking, he never wore anything else. The boy was in his jeans and fleece jacket. They walked with their heads down, the boy with his hands stuck in his jacket pockets, the uncle with his hands by his side and his dark hair falling over his forehead. As he stepped through her door, he gave her a shy smile that was not returned. The uncle ordered a BLT for himself and a ham sandwich for his nephew.

"Okay," he said, as Faith walked away. She was in the kitchen when the uncle asked the boy if he knew what a selkie was. The boy shook his head and the uncle told him it was a mythical creature that resembles a seal in the water, but a human on land.

"Are they real?" the boy said.

"Of course they are. Sean married one."

"Whose Sean?"

There was a pause before the uncle said, "A fisherman."

The boy looked out the window towards the river.

The uncle started to tell him about the three fishermen coming along the coast one evening. The sun was just about to set and they were hungry and tired and looking forward to getting home. Sean was the first around a bend in the road. He stopped so suddenly that the others bumped into him and the three stared at the most beautiful woman they had ever seen. Sean said that she was a selkie. Look, there's her skin lying on the rock beside her.

The boy was watching his uncle with a frown. He was not so tight in the shoulders, but his hands were hidden under the table and gave the impression that he would have liked to hide. The uncle had his jacket off and the rolled up shirt sleeves gave him the look of determination or settling into a task he wasn't sure he was capable of, though he seemed more at ease when he thanked Faith for the sandwiches.

"Sean's friend agreed that it had to be a selkie," the uncle said after he took a first bite of the sandwich. Faith had retreated to the counter and pretended to be busy with menus. Her gaze was constantly pulled to the table. A blue sky pushed against the window and the boy ate in small tidy bites.

"So Sean crept forward and grabbed the seal's skin. He held it tightly with both hands when the woman looked up with a sad expression on her face. Will you not give me back my skin? she asked sadly."

Faith was staring at the uncle now. His hair was growing long. There was a boyish excitement in the way he leaned forward. The uncle told the boy that selkies were supposed to make the best wives and Sean wanted her to be his, so he said no he wouldn't give back the skin. The selkie said she would miss the sea but she had no choice.

The boy's mouth had opened. He took a sip of his Fanta. Everything he did was slow and thoughtful.

The uncle continued, "They were married three days later and Sean locked the selkies skin in a chest and kept the key around his neck. Sean's fortunes improved as soon as he was married and in no time he owned his own fishing fleet. His wife gave him three strong sons and two beautiful daughters. Sean was very happy, but his wife spent as much time as she could by the sea with her own people. Eventually Sean decided that his family had to move to a bigger house. The day they were leaving, Sean's wife went into the house to take a last look around. In one corner, she noticed the chest. It was so old it was easy to break the lid. She couldn't believe her luck when she found her skin. She ran out the door and raced down to the sea. She heard Sean chasing after her and shouting his love. But, before he could catch up, she threw on her skin. In front of his eyes, she changed back into her seal form and swam far out to sea."

The silence was thick and seemed to descend on the boy. He was watching his uncle.

"What happened?" the nephew finally said. The uncle shook his head. When he glanced at Faith, she dropped her gaze. She would have known the end of the story: the selkie disappeared and never came back.

The boy's dark eyes searched his uncle's.

"Sean moved to his house," the uncle said, and Faith looked helplessly at the boy. She probably wanted to tell the boy that the selkie came back every week to visit her family and everyone was happy, but it wasn't true, so she was left to look at the two figures at the small table so alike in their falling posture and dark hair, yet miles apart from each other.

We didn't think it was anger that kept her baking all night, but a heavy regret that wouldn't let her sit still. She phoned her kitchen porter in the morning to help her clean up and he whistled when he saw the piles of cakes along the sideboards, 'Chocolate Pound Cakes, Banana cakes, Neapolitan cheese cake, Confetti cakes with Chocolate Filling and Ginger bread men were only the half of it. Once again, she got to the church before mass and asked the priest to announce a cake sale. She was the first to walk out with her head held high and chocolate sauce on her cheek. There were more customers than the week before. Children played outside hopping off the pavement as we fought for our cakes. We quieted down when we saw the boy's mother arrive holding the boy's hand. She was tall and broad-shouldered with short greying hair and a reluctant smile. She bought ginger bread men.

The uncle did not come.

"Don't you like cakes?" Faith said the next week. The window seat was taken and the table by the wall made the boy and uncle look caged in. He looked surprised. His dark eyes lingered on her a moment before he said he did, but he didn't like early mass. "Will the cake sale be every Sunday?" he said.

She said it might.

The orders were taken. We were nervous to hear what story the uncle might share. With each one he seemed to be digging a hole for himself, taking the boy further away, but it was hard to imagine the uncle doing anything else.

When he started to tell the boy about the giant Finn McCool in the North and his on-going feud with the Scottish giant Benandonner, Faith smiled. It was impossible to think a boy would dislike this story. The uncle said, "Benandonner wanted to fight Finn and crossed the sea for him. The whole land shock with his steps and Finn and his wife Oonagh knew it was a battle he would never win."

"How big was he?"

"As big as two houses..."

"And how big was Finn?"

There was a pause. Faith, getting the sandwiches missed the uncle's shrug. "As big as one house..."

The boy said oh.

"When the giant got to Ireland, he roared for Finn. Oonagh ran out to him and asked him to hush now. "Be quiet, my baby is in bed."

At the table, the boy was sitting straight. His chair was an inch from the table and his head was cocked. He didn't look at Faith when she slid the plates on the table. The uncle's narrow shoulders were bent over the table. He said that Oonagh had gotten Finn to lie in the cot and pretend to be their baby. When Benandonner saw the size of the baby he got a bit of a shock. The boy laughed.

"Oonagh invited him to stay for lunch," the uncle went on. "She'd baked bread with stones and said it was her husband's favorite. But once Benandonner ate some three of his teeth broke. The poor fella needed to clear his head after that and Oonagh brought him outside where the garden was scattered with boulders as big as the giant. Finn likes to play catch with those boulders she said. He flings them over the Fort and runs to catch them before they land. Benandonner tried to lift one but could barely get it up an inch. He was scared of Finn then, because he could eat stones for lunch and throw boulders miles and had a baby half the size of Benandonner himself, so he thanked Oonagh for her hospitality and said he needed to get back before the tide turned."

Silence, and the boy said, "Did he ever came back?"

"Not that I know of," said the uncle.

"But what if he came back," the boy was sitting forward with wide-eyed worry. Faith saw his hands were gripping the arm rest.

She stepped forward. "They'll be friends if he comes back," Faith said.

The porter was at the kitchen door, but he probably wouldn't have noticed the boy's grasp easing, the stiffness of Faith's legs, or the gratitude in the uncle's eyes.

"They won't fight?" the nephew asked her.

She said, "No, they won't fight."

Now we could tell you about the weeks of stories that followed and the cakes Faith continued to bake on Saturday nights and her growing pride as she walked out of mass on Sunday mornings. But we don't recall the particulars of the stories or how long it took before Faith stopped doing sandwiches to concentrate on what she loved. She kept the kitchen porter on and he surprised her with how well he took to baking, but that is beside the point. What is important is that before the bakery took off and people started traveling from miles around, the uncle and nephew stopped coming. Faith spent two Saturdays standing at the café counter until her legs grew stiff. There was a good reason for their failure to come, the nephew took ill and was unable to leave the house, or the mother decided to get away for a while and left with her son. We don't recall the specifics, no one does. It was the sight of Faith Wheeler sitting in her bright café late at night that people still talk about. With the light shining over her, she was as still as a statue. No one knew she was waiting until the uncle walked through her door and she stood for him. The street was quiet then, not a soul in sight, so we are not sure who was the first to see Faith Wheeler and Dick Hurley embrace, but there must have been a witness.

About Fomite

A fomite is a medium capable of transmitting infectious organisms from one individual to another.

"The activity of art is based on the capacity of people to be infected by the feelings of others." Tolstoy, *What Is Art?*

Writing a review on Amazon, Good Reads, Shelfari, Library Thing or other social media sites for readers will help the progress of independent publishing. To submit a review, go to the book page on any of the sites and follow the links for reviews. Books from independent presses rely on reader to reader communications.

For more information or to order any of our books, visit
http://www.fomitepress.com/FOMITE/Our_Books.html

More Titles from Fomite...

Novels

Joshua Amses — *During This, Our Nadir*
Joshua Amses — *Ghatsr*
Joshua Amses — *Raven or Crow*
Joshua Amses — *The Moment Before an Injury*
Jaysinh Birjepatel — *Nothing Beside Remains*
Jaysinh Birjepatel — *The Good Muslim of Jackson Heights*
David Brizer — *Victor Rand*
Paula Closson Buck — *Summer on the Cold War Planet*
Dan Chodorkoff — *Loisaida*
David Adams Cleveland — *Time's Betrayal*
Jaimee Wriston Colbert — *Vanishing Acts*
Roger Coleman — *Skywreck Afternoons*
Marc Estrin — *Hyde*
Marc Estrin — *Kafka's Roach*
Marc Estrin — *Speckled Vanities*
Zdravka Evtimova — *In the Town of Joy and Peace*

Fomite

Zdravka Evtimova — *Sinfonia Bulgarica*
Daniel Forbes — *Derail This Train Wreck*
Greg Guma — *Dons of Time*
Richard Hawley — *The Three Lives of Jonathan Force*
Lamar Herrin — *Father Figure*
Michael Horner — *Damage Control*
Ron Jacobs — *All the Sinners Saints*
Ron Jacobs — *Short Order Frame Up*
Ron Jacobs — *The Co-conspirator's Tale*
Scott Archer Jones — *And Throw Away the Skins*
Scott Archer Jones — *A Rising Tide of People Swept Away*
Julie Justicz — *Degrees of Difficulty*
Maggie Kast — *A Free Unsullied Land*
Darrell Kastin — *Shadowboxing with Bukowski*
Coleen Kearon — *#triggerwarning*
Coleen Kearon — *Feminist on Fire*
Jan English Leary — *Thicker Than Blood*
Diane Lefer — *Confessions of a Carnivore*
Rob Lenihan — *Born Speaking Lies*
Douglas Milliken — *Our Shadow's Voice*
Colin Mitchell — *Roadman*
Ilan Mochari — *Zinsky the Obscure*
Peter Nash — *Parsimony*
Peter Nash — *The Perfection of Things*
George Ovitt — Stillpoint
George Ovitt — Tribunal
Gregory Papadoyiannis — *The Baby Jazz*
Pelham — *The Walking Poor*
Andy Potok — *My Father's Keeper*
Frederick Ramey — *Comes A Time*
Joseph Rathgeber — *Mixedbloods*
Kathryn Roberts — *Companion Plants*
Robert Rosenberg — *Isles of the Blind*
Fred Russell — *Rafi's World*
Ron Savage — *Voyeur in Tangier*
David Schein — *The Adoption*

Fomite

Lynn Sloan — *Principles of Navigation*
L.E. Smith — *The Consequence of Gesture*
L.E. Smith — *Travers' Inferno*
L.E. Smith — *Untimely RIPped*
Bob Sommer — *A Great Fullness*
Tom Walker — *A Day in the Life*
Susan V. Weiss —*My God, What Have We Done?*
Peter M. Wheelwright — *As It Is On Earth*
Suzie Wizowaty — *The Return of Jason Green*

Poetry

Anna Blackmer — *Hexagrams*
Antonello Borra — *Alfabestiario*
Antonello Borra — *AlphaBetaBestiaro*
Antonello Borra — *Fabbrica delle idee/The Factory of Ideas*
L. Brown — *Loopholes*
Sue D. Burton — *Little Steel*
David Cavanagh— *Cycling in Plato's Cave*
James Connolly — *Picking Up the Bodies*
Greg Delanty — *Loosestrife*
Mason Drukman — *Drawing on Life*
J. C. Ellefson — *Foreign Tales of Exemplum and Woe*
Tina Escaja/Mark Eisner — *Caida Libre/Free Fall*
Anna Faktorovich — *Improvisational Arguments*
Barry Goldensohn — *Snake in the Spine, Wolf in the Heart*
Barry Goldensohn — *The Hundred Yard Dash Man*
Barry Goldensohn — *The Listener Aspires to the Condition of Music*
R. L. Green — *When You Remember Deir Yassin*
Gail Holst-Warhaft — *Lucky Country*
Raymond Luczak — *A Babble of Objects*
Kate Magill — *Roadworthy Creature, Roadworthy Craft*
Tony Magistrale — *Entanglements*
Gary Mesick — *General Discharge*
Andreas Nolte — *Mascha: The Poems of Mascha Kaléko*
Sherry Olson — *Four-Way Stop*
Brett Ortler — *Lessons of the Dead*

Fomite

Aristea Papalexandrou/Philip Ramp — *Μας προσπερνά/It's Overtaking Us*
Janice Miller Potter — *Meanwell*
Janice Miller Potter — *Thoreau's Umbrella*
Philip Ramp — *The Melancholy of a Life as the Joy of Living It Slowly Chills*
Joseph D. Reich — *A Case Study of Werewolves*
Joseph D. Reich — *Connecting the Dots to Shangrila*
Joseph D. Reich — *The Derivation of Cowboys and Indians*
Joseph D. Reich — *The Hole That Runs Through Utopia*
Joseph D. Reich — *The Housing Market*
Kenneth Rosen and Richard Wilson — *Gomorrah*
Fred Rosenblum — *Vietnumb*
David Schein — *My Murder and Other Local News*
Harold Schweizer — *Miriam's Book*
Scott T. Starbuck — *Carbonfish Blues*
Scott T. Starbuck — *Hawk on Wire*
Scott T. Starbuck — *Industrial Oz*
Seth Steinz r — *Among the Lost*
Seth Steinzor — *To Join the Lost*
Susan Thomas — *In the Sadness Museum*
Susan Thomas — *The Empty Notebook Interrogates Itself*
Paolo Valesio/Todd Portnowitz — *La Mezzanotte di Spoleto/Midnight in Spoleto*
Sharon Webster — *Everyone Lives Here*
Tony Whedon — *The Tres Riches Heures*
Tony Whedon — *The Falkland Quartet*
Claire Zoghb — *Dispatches from Everest*

Stories

Jay Boyer — *Flight*
L. M Brown — *Treading the Uneven Road*
Michael Cocchiarale — *Here Is Ware*
Michael Cocchiarale — *Still Time*
Neil Connelly — *In the Wake of Our Vows*
Catherine Zobal Dent — *Unfinished Stories of Girls*
Zdravka Evtimova — *Carts and Other Stories*
John Michael Flynn — *Off to the Next Wherever*
Derek Furr — *Semitones*

Fomite

Derek Furr — *Suite for Three Voices*
Elizabeth Genovise — *Where There Are Two or More*
Andrei Guriuanu — *Body of Work*
Zeke Jarvis — *In A Family Way*
Arya Jenkins — *Blue Songs in an Open Key*
Jan English Leary — *Skating on the Vertical*
Marjorie Maddox — *What She Was Saying*
William Marquess — *Boom-shacka-lacka*
Gary Miller — *Museum of the Americas*
Jennifer Anne Moses — *Visiting Hours*
Martin Ott — *Interrogations*
Christopher Peterson — *Amoebic Simulacra*
Jack Pulaski — *Love's Labours*
Charles Rafferty — *Saturday Night at Magellan's*
Ron Savage — *What We Do For Love*
Fred Skolnik— *Americans and Other Stories*
Lynn Sloan — *This Far Is Not Far Enough*
L.E. Smith — *Views Cost Extra*
Caitlin Hamilton Summie — *To Lay To Rest Our Ghosts*
Susan Thomas — *Among Angelic Orders*
Tom Walker — *Signed Confessions*
Silas Dent Zobal — *The Inconvenience of the Wings*

Odd Birds

William Benton — *Eye Contact: Writing on Art*
Micheal Breiner — *the way none of this happened*
J. C. Ellefson — *Under the Influence: Shouting Out to Walt*
David Ross Gunn — *Cautionary Chronicles*
Andrei Guriuanu and Teknari — *The Darkest City*
Gail Holst-Warhaft — *The Fall of Athens*
Roger Lebovitz — *A Guide to the Western Slopes and the Outlying Area*
Roger Lebovitz — *Twenty-two Instructions for Near Survival*
dug Nap— *Artsy Fartsy*
Delia Bell Robinson — *A Shirtwaist Story*
Peter Schumann — *Belligerent & Not So Belligerent Slogans from the Possibilitarian Arsenal*

Peter Schumann — *Bread & Sentences*
Peter Schumann — *Charlotte Salomon*
Peter Schumann — *Diagonal Man Theory + Praxis, Volumes One and Two*
Peter Schumann — *Faust 3*
Peter Schumann — *Planet Kasper, Volumes One and Two*
Peter Schumann — *We*

Plays
Stephen Goldberg — *Screwed and Other Plays*
Michele Markarian — *Unborn Children of America*

Essays
Robert Sommer — *Losing Francis: Essays on the Wars at Home*